Late to Breakfast

Laura Rudacille

Year of the Book Press
Glen Rock, Pennsylvania

ISBN: 978-1-942430-03-2

Library of Congress Control Number: 2014956968

This is a work of fiction. Names, characters, places, and incidents either are the product of the author's imagination or are used fictitiously. Any resemblance to actual events or locales or persons, living or dead, is entirely coincidental.

Printed in the United States of America

Unearth happiness, exploit joy,
and consume possibility at every turn...
...Possibilities Are My Favorite.
L.

Acknowledgements

Grace and gratitude to:

~ My family, Adam, Mason, and especially Teague, for grounding me during the final drafts. "You're overthinking it." And my personal favorite, "I know your book is romance and I haven't had firsthand experience with relationships yet, but I can help you strengthen your plot."

~ My mom, Gene, for continued encouragement and painstaking editing. I truly couldn't have unearthed the diamond without you.

~ Demi Stevens of *Year of the Book* for growth, knowledge, and support throughout my writing process. You're a beacon for indies navigating this ever-changing industry. YOTBpress.com

~ Cheers to Happily Ever After – Thank you Jenn Lynch and Jon Stiles for saying YES to each other and then to me! I am so grateful for your generosity in sharing your engagement photo for my cover.

~ PHILTER photography, Camp Hill, PA, photographer Harmony Boore. Thank you for capturing the sun!
www.philterphoto.com, www.philtergallery.com, www.facebook.com/philterphoto.

~ Jane Yost Photography of York, PA, for brilliant editing of my dream photo. www.janeyost/smugmug/com

~ Pre-readers Carin, Carol, Christine, K2, Kristen, Pam, Tina, and Tonya ~ I appreciate you refraining from red pen usage as I fine-tuned my manuscript. Your insights enhanced and brightened my words until they shined.

~ My biggest thank you is for my readers and *Saltwater Cowboy* fans. I appreciate your patience and value your support. I hope you enjoy *Late to Breakfast!*

CHAPTER ONE

Tory lifted the copper kettle before the steam whistle screamed and shattered the stillness of the house. She squeezed the jaws of the steeping spoon, filled the casing with loose tea leaves, then placed it in the belly of a hand-thrown mug. Scalding water drowned the metal. The heady scent of mint wafted into the air, encircling her like a lifelong friend. She added a splash of milk and too much sugar, then padded across the hardwood.

She hated to complain. No one would hear her anyway, the house was empty.

The symphony of the house surrounded her. The walls and windows popped in staccato percussion as they relinquished the heat of the day. The soft chimes of the mantle clock supplied a beckoning melody.

In the foyer, the dogs, Remi and Poncho, waited. "Hello, girls and boys." Tails tattooed a pattern of greeting. Tory avoided paws and tails and maneuvered around their lounging bodies to double check the lock on the front door. "How about we make an effort to share the mattress tonight?" At her invitation the dogs raced to the second floor.

She gripped the newel post and smiled at the rise of wood. How many times had she and her brother straddled the banister and slid from the top all the way to the bottom? Their playful shenanigans were often met by a stern look from their mother, while over her shoulder their grandfather would wink and tell them if they'd oil the wood they'd go faster.

The planks grumbled beneath Tory's feet like the hips of the elderly. Each tread reminded her how weary she was.

The veterinary conference was approaching fast. Not a vet herself, Tory was scheduled to present the benefits of equine therapeutic massage. On top of the conference, it was almost foaling season. Throughout the next eight weeks, new life would bless her Montana ranch. The unpredictability of labor and delivery would make busy schedules hectic in the most perfect of ways. In addition to the birthing, the summer house was under construction. Contractors and carpenters scurried about making noise more suitable for suburbia than the serene mountain-shadowed ranch. And to make matters more demanding Murphy, her brother and co-owner of Keen Ranch, was out of town.

Tonight Tory would embrace tranquility – a hot bath, an intriguing book, and a solid eight hours of sleep. She walked the long hallway to the bathroom, settled her tea on the shelf, and spun the tap on the antique claw-foot tub. She selected a jar of scented bath salts, and sprinkled an indulgent handful into the flow before stepping out of her clothes. The rising mist infused the chilly air with an aromatic punch of vanilla and jasmine.

She gathered her mass of hair on top of her head and eased into the frothy water. Bubbles tickled her chin. Moist heat soothed muscle and bone. Tory leaned her head against the porcelain and made an effort to calm her swirling mind.

Her skin was pink and pruney, her teacup half empty. She smelled of flowers and felt every inch pampered and female. Tory climbed from the tub, toweled off, and opened the anti-aging lotion a friend had given her for her birthday.

"Anti-aging," she snorted and slathered it over her skin.

Tory cast a look into the full length mirror. No longer willowy, as she'd been in her teens, her body was toned from hard work rather than a membership-required facility and at twenty-seven supported the curvature expected in a woman. Her thick hair, rich and red, drifted across her shoulders. Copper tips dangled well below her collarbone. Tory grabbed a fistful and analyzed the ends. She was overdue for a trim. "Another line on the to-do list." She shrugged into her robe, then lifted the remains of her tea. Her cell phone alert sounded.

A glimpse at the text had Tory shifting gears like a racecar driver on Sunday. Terrycloth dropped in a heap. Fingers worked like a master weaver to secure damp hair into an intricate braid. Clothes shed moments before were tugged in place. Tory bolted down the steps. Sock covered feet disappeared into knee high boots as she lifted her coat from the peg. She threaded arms into sleeves, and drew the zipper from hip to neck and surged into the night.

Tory hesitated before climbing into her rig. She tipped her face to the vast Montana sky and breathed the crisp unblemished air. Stars winked and generously offered the burst of fortitude she needed.

Whatever faced her, disgust, despair, and on occasion death, rescuing neglected and abused animals was not for sissies.

CHAPTER TWO

Flashing lights painted the night sky with an unnatural wash of red and blue. Tory weaved with care through the property littered with garbage and scrap metal. She pulled her rig with a horse trailer in tandem to the side of the narrow road and set the brake.

The homestead was a patchwork of structures surrounding a small farmhouse. Outbuildings leaned like heavy-eyed children around a large barn. Emergency personnel and countless volunteers worked to access and coordinate the site. Tory climbed from the cab and entered the fray.

Buried in the middle of the chaos, looking more like a rodeo clown than the county vet, was Doc Webb. A lime green beanie perched atop wild curly tresses that rebelled and flirted with the collar of his buffalo plaid shirt. Threadbare elbows and frayed flannel tails ended at the hip pockets of ancient denim which hung loosely and disappeared into knee high muck boots.

As a young girl, Tory had fallen hard for the man who knew everything there was to know about the animals on the ranch. She'd marveled at Doc Webb's ability to gain the trust of the young, pacify the old, and mend the impossible. She'd shadowed him to the point of annoyance but he'd never shushed her away. On her sixteenth birthday, Doc Webb had come to her party saddened from an emergency call. An elderly man had fallen into bad health and could no longer care for his livestock. Doc Webb had felt compelled to relocate the animals to caring farms as soon as possible. Tory leapt at the chance to pitch in.

With her Nana's help, Tory reached out to neighboring farms and within a few days all the animals were adopted. Her efforts drew the attention of the local media. The project spurred Tory to action. She designated a corral at the rear of the Keen Ranch where animals could recoup and regain their zest for living while she found them deserving homes.

Over the years Tory's passion expanded to include educational programs for people of all ages. She taught responsible livestock ownership, stable care, grooming, and riding lessons.

Tory approached Doc Webb as he dictated the facts into his compact recorder. "Three counts cruelty and endangerment. Digitally documented witness statements and scene on record. Immediate emergency medical seizure – two goats – critical condition. Immediate endangerment seizure – mare – serious condition. Assessment in progress. Preliminary recommendation – relocation of remaining livestock pending hearing."

Doc Webb clicked the device off, "There's my girl." He organized the stack of papers and set the file and recorder on the seat of the truck. "Sorry to hijack your beauty hours, but it's only fair to allow the rest of the ladies of the world to gain some ground." He reached behind the seat and produced two thermal mugs of coffee.

Tory wiggled her fingers like a greedy child. She sipped the sweetened, lightened caffeine and tried not to whimper. "Thank you, thank you, thank you."

"Least I can do."

A small cluster of college volunteers milled about the property. For the past year Doc Webb had been guest lecturing at the local university. His students adored him. In an effort to please their professor they had begun to show up and assist during rescues.

"I see your groupies made the party," Tory jabbed him with a good-humored elbow.

"What can I say? They love me," he shrugged. "I'd really like you to meet Avery. He's here somewhere."

"The golden boy," Tory muttered. Avery had been Doc Webb's intern for the last two weeks. She had yet to cross paths with him. Doc Webb was forever singing Avery's praises. Tory felt there was no need to meet the man in person.

"I think he's the one."

"So you continue to say." Tory focused on her coffee. She didn't want to consider a time when Doc Webb would stop working. The man barely took a day off. What would he do with endless hours, days and weeks in a row?

"I convinced him to cover the clinic for the next two weeks, until I'm back from my trip."

"Trip?" Tory sputtered and turned her full attention to Doc Webb.

"Takin' the Mrs. on that cruise I've been promising her. Married forty years."

"Forgot about that." Tory leaned against his truck. She tried for a moment to picture him in board-shorts, a floppy hat, with his nose painted with florescent zinc. Considering his usual haphazard wardrobe, she imagined it could work. But the why of it baffled her. Vacation was as fickle an idea as retirement.

Shouts and curses sliced through the air. Tory spared a glance toward a handcuffed man being led to the awaiting police cruiser. He twisted against his restraints, face contorted with rage as vile threats pierced anyone within reach.

"Owner isn't happy."

"Nope." Doc Webb rested his fists on his hips and rolled his neck from side to side. "And considering the idiot shoved a first responder, his fun is just beginning."

"Ignorance."

"With a cherry on top." He shrugged, "Until the domesticated animals become predatory and fight back with fangs and claws, fines and citations are the best we can do."

Tory sighed. "What do you need from me?"

"Take on a horse, a mare, approximately two years old." He leaned companionably beside her. "She has an infected lesion, left front leg. She's understandably skittish, and in desperate need of a bath." He patted his pockets in search of his ever present pack of Wrigley's. "Give her the Tory special, nutrition, love and once she'll allow it, a bit of your magic fingers." His lips twitched in a playful smile as he offered her a piece of gum.

"No problem." She folded the spearmint rectangle into her mouth.

"The two goats however," Doc Webb grimaced and folded his wrapper into tiny triangles. "They'll need a full-blown miracle. I'm taking them directly to surgery."

A police officer interrupted and told them they were cleared to begin the livestock seizure.

Their banter ended as Doc Webb walked toward the barn. He muttered a curse as he lifted his leg to clear the jagged edges of a rusted fifty-gallon drum. "I know you're tough, but I need you to be prepared."

Pungent aroma of rotting straw and mounds of manure saturated the air. Tory tugged the bandana around her neck over her nose and mouth as she entered the dimly lit barn.

In the far corner a small lifeless body lay. Across the enclosure two more goats huddled together in the putrid bedding. Their coats showed signs of disease, but the obvious injuries were to their front legs. Broken bones prevented them from standing erect. Their bodies tipped forward at awkward angles, their heads dangled in defeat.

"Good Heavens," Tory pressed her hand to her stomach. "Can they be saved?"

"I'll do my best." He accepted a blanket from a tech and entered the pen. "The mare's behind the barn. Take charge with her, evaluate and transport her to your place." He lowered his voice as he moved carefully toward the pair. "I'll check with you later."

Tory watched a moment longer. The trembling goats fixed their shock-glazed eyes on Doc Webb. He knelt alongside the brown and white nanny, ran his hand over her face before swaddling her in a warming blanket and lifting her into his arms. Tory would have sworn the goat melted into his embrace. It was magic to observe Doc Webb in action. She only hoped he had enough pixie dust to remedy their wounds.

Anger pushed against the pity and threatened to strangle her. It never got easier to witness the accomplishments of blatant ignorance. She strode from the barn, and drew the cloth off her face. Against the stark impeccable black Montana sky, sanguine stars continued to glitter. Tory filed the goats and the agony of their condition away. Time to focus on the mare.

A course of barbed wire linked trees, discarded metal, and shards of wood. The excuse of a paddock was too small for a full grown horse. A gasp whooshed past her lips as Tory's gaze settled on the young mare standing against a splintered shed. Her head dangled low. Whether she lacked strength or desire to raise it was unclear.

Tory assessed the young horse. Her filth encrusted body obscured the color of her coat. Inches of knots and snarls riddled her mane and tail. But worse, was the angry red wound on her front leg, where the open flesh gaped and oozed.

Tory gave a curt nod to a man leaning against the wire fence. His tattered hoodie and ripped jeans screamed college co-ed. "You one of Doc Webb's minions?"

"I suppose."

"My rig," Tory dug her hand deep into her front pocket. "Bring it around." In a deliberate move she tossed her keys. He nipped the ring out of the air an instant before the metal impacted his nose. "And fetch the canvas tote, halter and lead from behind the seat." Tory unfastened the gate and stepped inside the enclosure.

He looked at the keys cradled in his palm, then back at the woman who had ordered and dismissed him without even asking his name, and then wandered off to locate her truck.

The soft mud and manure gripped Tory's boot like quicksand. The mare's tail swished hard to the side. "You don't want me in your space, I know..." Tory pacified as she navigated the muck. "I'm going to take you some place beautiful. Would you like that?"

The mare tossed her head and shifted her weight. Tory took a tentative stride forward. Her smooth tone had the horse's ears perking.

She heard the rumble of her truck. Sensing her helper, Tory extended her hand behind her. "Give me the halter and the lead. Set the satchel by the gate." She waited for the woven strap to hit her palm. "Thanks. Now go be helpful somewhere else."

"We're going to be friends." Tory inched forward, little by little, raised a hand, and stroked the dirty muzzle. "That-a-girl." She slipped the halter over the mare's head and snapped the lead in place.

A grin of triumph bloomed. She flicked a glance over her shoulder to share the victory with her helper. Her smile dimmed when she found herself beaming at an apple. With a shrug Tory returned her attention to her charge. "I did tell him to go, didn't I?" The mare snorted, making her laugh. "I'm just surprised he listened."

Tory threaded out a few feet of slack, stretched toward the gate, and grabbed the apple. "He left you a treat." Curiosity sparked in the young horse's eyes. "Hungry?" Tory bit a chunk from the scarlet fruit.

The horse's nostrils flared. Her body tensed with intent of an entirely different motivation. Extending her neck, seeking the source of the sweet fragrance, the mare closed the distance until she nipped the apple from Tory's palm.

Ribbons of pink and gold had begun to chase away the dark. The curtain was rising. Spring was in the air. Just the smallest hint in the wind as Mother Nature prepared to shift gears.

"I bet beneath those layers of muck you're a princess." The mare tossed her head regally despite her tattered mane and mud caked coat. "I was always partial to Ariel," Tory giggled. "Will you sprout fins when I hose you down?" The horse nudged Tory's hip seeking more treats.

"Let's get you home. We don't want to be late for breakfast."

Avery bit back the laugh rooted in his throat. "Go be helpful somewhere else." He'd never been so effectively dismissed.

The moment he'd seen her step from the barn Avery had been struck by the war of emotions on her face. He'd been captivated by the shift from anguish to fierce determination as her long legs consumed the ground. Each resolute stride sent her blaze of braided hair swinging like a pendulum mid-spine.

He'd seen. He'd watched, and he'd known…Tory Keen.

As a grad student Avery had learned about Tory Keen. Since taking the internship with Doc Webb two weeks ago, he'd heard more. More than any man hoping to make his own mark in the field of animal care wanted to hear. She was brilliant, strong willed, and independent. If you asked Doc Webb, Tory was the Equine *Mother Teresa* – a trailblazer for large animal abuse, an educator and a pioneer for the benefits of equine therapeutic massage. When Tory Keen spoke, people listened.

Avery had pictured her older and tougher in look and physique. He hadn't expected miles of leg stilting a tightly toned body, hair like fire, and a face that weakened the knee.

"Avery," Doc Webb rushed from the barn. "Just the man I need."

For the second time in a matter of minutes Avery caught a flying set of keys.

"The goats are stabilized, but we need to get them into surgery pronto. Get us to the clinic."

CHAPTER THREE

Tory stood inside the mudroom and allowed the magic of the Keen homestead to soak in. The soundtrack from *Mamma Mia* was playing, coffee was brewing, and if her nose was on point, Belgian waffles were browning. God bless Ginny.

Ginny, the seventy-year-old ruler of the Keen kitchen, had been Tory's Nana's best friend. Although cooking was her primary function, 'Cook' was about as understated a job description you could place on her.

"Morning, Tory love." Ginny rested her hand on her hip. "You ever come to my kitchen late I'll know you've been up to no good." Her eyes scanned Tory from head to toe. "Although," her lips pursed, "you've been up to something. You're wearing the same clothes as yesterday." The girl was pale. Worry tinted her cheeks like morbid foundation. Ginny pulled a mug from the cupboard and filled it with the herbal tea Tory preferred after her morning jolt of coffee. She handed Tory the fragrant liquid. "From the look of you, the rescue was bad." Ginny nudged Tory toward the foyer. "Grab a shower and try to fool yourself into thinking the past hours were a dream."

"A nightmare," Tory mumbled as she scaled the stairs but decided not to spoil Ginny's morning with details.

She tossed fresh jeans and a cable knit sweater on her tidily dressed bed. How she'd love to fold the quilt over and crawl into lush comfort. A circular saw sputtered then screamed to life ending her fantasy. "Like an electric guitar in church," Tory grumbled and shifted to the window to look over the progress of the cottage renovation.

A little over a year ago Tory had forced her brother to take a vacation. She expected him to come home with a fresh perspective and a tan. But Murphy had returned with an attractive woman, Jess, and her young son, Riley.

The patter of a budding family stretched their living arrangements to maximum. Tory knew, despite how much she adored Jess, two women under the same roof making a home was more estrogen than bricks and mortar could sustain.

Through the pane Tory assessed. The workers were ahead of schedule. A good cleaning, a few coats of interior paint, and she'd be sliding furniture into place.

More items for her to-do list.

Feeling human, Tory jogged the last half of the staircase and pushed through the galley doors.

Ginny's spatula flourished. She conducted the ingredients in her skillet like a seasoned orchestra. Beside her, lead ranch hand, Dale, reclined against the sink, gripping a mug of coffee. The pair were as vital to the Keen Ranch as the stone foundation beneath Tory's feet.

"There's our girl," Dale smiled at Tory. "Mare's settled," he said before she could ask. "I put her in the circular corral, and gave her a bit of sweet feed."

"Ariel," Tory hitched her hip on a stool. "I named her Ariel."

"Lovely," Ginny donned mitts and removed a tray of thick waffles from the oven. "The mermaid, that's just lovely." She placed the steaming carbohydrates in front of Tory, picked up the syrup, and doused the golden edges. "You've done what you can to care for those you could help. Now eat." She lifted a plate from the cupboard and stacked it high for Dale. "You too." She motioned him to a stool alongside Tory. "Take a moment, fuel up before you tackle the rest of your day."

The phone rang. Tory frowned at the vintage contraption hanging on the wall. The strident sound confirmed the rescue had made the morning news. "Don't answer it."

"You know I must," Ginny turned her palms out. "Dale and I have a wager going."

Tory scowled. The phone would ring for the next several days. Busybodies seeking morsels to season the week's gossip, and others who would offer monetary help toward the animals' care and veterinary expenses. "How do they sniff us out so quickly?"

"It's their job, I'd say." Dale wiped his mouth and pushed his plate aside. Ginny replaced the receiver and marked a tally on the chalkboard. "Yes!" Dale pumped his fist in the air.

Tory's narrowed gaze sent Dale scurrying to the barn.

"What type of wager?" Tory asked Ginny.

"Dale said you'd have donations, inquiries for lessons, and a follow-up reporter before ten."

"And you?"

"I said those were a given. My money's on local television wanting a live report from the ranch and the Rescue League hitting you for personal face time at the State Fair."

Tory's belly rolled. "I have no time for nonsense." She shoved to her feet. "Thanks for breakfast, Ginny. I'll be in the barn if you need me. I'll be in Iceland if a reporter shows up."

Avery drove along the weathered dirt lane leading to the Keen Ranch. The two-story home was surrounded by stables and riding rings, and was accented by a canvas-worthy backdrop of distant snow tipped mountains. A Google search had filled in the human details. Grandparents, building from the basics, forged a legacy which they passed to Tory and her brother. The third generation had branched out to include horses and animal advocacy adding layers to the ranch's impeccable reputation.

Avery glanced at the clock in the console. It was after one. The procedure on the goats had taken several hours. Both lives had been saved...for the moment. Doc Webb sent him to collect preliminary paperwork on the mare from Tory. The documentation and facts would add strength to their legal case. Avery had to admit he had little knowledge of this facet of the veterinary world. He expected in his permanent position in Maryland, he'd see even less. Surgeons generally fixed what was broken and moved to the next patient. Not unlike the human world where orthopedic specialists repaired the bones and tendons leaving therapists and general practitioners to stay the course of healing.

Avery spotted Dale talking with a bunch of men by the small cottage. His stomach growled when he noticed open lunch coolers. His night of caffeine and candy bars had been followed by a bagged snack from the vending machine paired with a Mountain Dew. Fourteen hours of the dietary choices of a teenager – no wonder he was hungry.

Dale lifted a hand in greeting and walked toward Avery. "Hell of a way to start your day." He held out a sub. "Roast beef and Swiss?"

Avery could have keeled over. "If those guys knew me better, I'd kiss you."

Dale slapped Avery hard on the shoulder. "Let me introduce you, then you can pucker up."

CHAPTER FOUR

The midday sun was high overhead. The breeze off the mountains ruffled the tails of Tory's work shirt. She popped the twine on a fresh bale of hay. Shadows raced over the fields where fences cordoned the acres of grazing land. Horses of all ages nibbled the spring green grass. In a few weeks foals would join their mothers and begin their lives in the shade of the mountains. The *Circle of Life* theme from *Lion King* filled Tory's mind. The promise of new beginnings.

The rescues were in various stages of recovery. "Another beautiful day in picturesque Montana." The horses lifted their heads and whinnied. "You folks are sitting pretty. Fresh food and water, soft straw at your feet."

Ariel stood alone in the middle of her round enclosure. She was clean and free of mud, her injured leg treated with antibiotic cream. She was one of the lucky ones. A few days longer and the infection on her leg would have festered and threatened her life.

"Check it out, Ariel. New friends for you."

Ariel's eyes, wide and curious, flicked toward the small group of horses in the pasture. Tory dropped a chunk of hay over the rail. Ariel's hooves shifted as her rumbling belly worked to overrule her trepidation.

"That's it, sweetie. No demons here. No one is lurking in the dark to sneak up on you in a tight stable and put their hands on you, or worse. You're safe. I promise." Ariel moseyed toward the fence, nudged the wedge of hay, then dug into her meal. "You'll have a new life here. I promise I will make it a happy one." Tory glanced toward the cottage. All was quiet for the moment as the work crew broke for lunch.

Across the gravel path Smooch, a rescued llama, lifted his head and trotted as close as the fence would allow. The ranch gigolo,

Smooch jutted his neck through the rails and thrust his fuzzy lips toward Tory. "Tell her, Smooch," she indulged the flirt by walking closer and bending down for his kiss. "Rewriting history is a Keen family tradition."

Tory remembered moving halfway across the nation to the ranch as a child. Her mother needed distance to recover from a broken marriage. The family accepted the sanctuary their grandparents' ranch offered and in time, they healed.

It had been the best decision all around, Tory realized as she grew older. Their mother had gotten her feet under her and blossomed like a flower in the meadow. Blooming so brightly she caught the eye of Edward and was now happily married and traveling the world. Tory and Murphy developed a bond of their own, working side by side as their grandparents poured every ounce of passion for horses and the land into them.

Tory loved the horses, but she had trouble not falling hard for each and every one. She glanced at Ariel and grinned. Good thing her brother was in Florida visiting Mickey Mouse. Tory was free to fuss and fall in love without prying eyes.

Saws and hammers roared to life. "Lunchtime is over, I guess." She shielded her eyes. When Tory had mentioned her plans to renovate the summer house she had been thinking on the line of updating the kitchen and modifying the practical bathroom. Murphy'd had other ideas. One call to their honorary brother Joel and a brilliant modification of the small structure emerged.

Her little cottage would be cozy and feminine and leave her independent from the main house, almost. An ingenious insulated glass breezeway met log and married with rustic stone connecting the two structures. Tory could picture herself seated in a rocking chair with her tea at the end of a long day, watching the sun set in brilliant bursts behind the mountains.

Men scrambled over the roof securing the new shingles. On the ground Dale stood, feet braced wide, fists on hips with a man she didn't recognize. They gestured toward the building discussing who knows what in a language of nods, grunts, and casual shrugs. Another carpenter she decided. Tall and fit, the kind of physique she'd be attracted to if she indulged in such frivolity.

A car bumped over the lane. The dogs surged to their feet and raced toward the house. Tory removed her leather gloves and glanced at her cell phone. The day's minutes were passing like the blur of an Olympic sprinter. Cora, Tory's favorite student was early, no surprise. The child would move into the stable if she were allowed.

CHAPTER FIVE

"Good control, Cora." Dressed in lime green riding pants, watermelon vest and a riding hat accented with powder blue polka dots, the little girl was a picture. Seeing the youngster seated atop Star, Tory's champion, not in blood line but in heart, was the balm Tory needed on a day like today.

Three years ago Tory had pulled Star from a ruin of a barn. His hip and rib bones protruded and stretched his hide like fabric across a weaving loom. It hadn't been a trouble-free recovery but treatment, medical and holistic, had prevailed and Star triumphed. The courts granted Keen Ranch permanent custody. During his recuperation Tory sensed gentleness in Star. With her guidance he had grown into one of Tory's best riding lesson horses.

"Bring him to an easy trot." Cora had amazing competency for an almost ten-year-old. "Perfect. Finish the circle then canter a figure eight, both directions. Be sure to change lead."

Tory looked on with pride in horse and rider. Cora executed a flawless change of gait. "Well done, Cora. Bring him in, cool him down and get him back into the barn."

"It can't be an hour already, Miss Tory." Cora whined as she always did at the conclusion of her lesson. "I just got here."

"Time flies, sweetie," Tory smiled. "What do you say you take an extra ten minutes? I'll text your Mom and tell her we're running late."

"You're the best."

Dale and the man he'd been talking with over lunch joined Tory along the rail. "Doesn't that make the sting of Ariel a bit easier to choke down?"

"Just thinking the same thing," Tory held the aluminum gate open for Cora and Star to pass through.

21

"We've a mare in the south pasture pre-labor," Dale said casually.

"Sweet Pea?" Tory opened her thermos and sipped cool water. "She's early. False labor?"

"Possible, it's her first." Dale hooked his thumbs in his front pockets waiting for Tory's instruction.

Her phone vibrated at her hip. She swiped her thumb across the screen. Tory's lips tightened as the voice of the president of the Equine Advocates filled her ear. She squeezed her eyes closed and cursed herself for not checking the caller ID.

"Yes...tragic...I know." Tory grabbed the tail of her braid and tugged. "You can imagine I'm very busy...Of course I realize with the news coverage we should..." She sighed. "I'm a bit short staffed at the moment... yes, it is important. I understand...I'll touch base next week." Tory snapped the phone closed and cursed. "Catch me when my defenses are down." She scuffed her boot in the dirt like a frustrated child. "Like I have an hour to dress up, paint my face, and solicit money from strangers."

"Illegal in this state, isn't it?" Dale quipped earning a snicker from the carpenter.

Tory's eyes flicked over the men. The amusement on their faces added to her irritation.

Dale squirmed, then cleared his throat.

"Relocate Sweat Pea to one of the rear stalls, extra bedding. We'll monitor her through the night in case she has trouble."

"I'd be happy to take a look at your mare, Miss Keen."

Tory snorted out a laugh. "Good one. Murphy would love it if I had the carpenter evaluate his laboring mare. Dale, settle Sweat Pea," she snapped. "And you," feral eyes cut to the workman. "Go nail something."

The men wisely remained silent as she marched toward the barn.

"She's um... an interesting woman."

"Balances more plates than the jugglers for Ringling Brothers." Dale thumped Avery between the shoulder blades. "Keeps me young, getting scolded when I haven't done anything wrong." Dale moved toward the pasture. "You'll see her bark has no teeth if you stick and get to know her."

"I'll risk the teeth and take a quick look at the mare."

Dale's brow lifted.

"In case Webb needs to stop out, later." Avery clarified.

As they crossed to the pasture Avery watched Tory disappear into the stable. Difficult to get to know someone who was always ordering and dismissing him, but he had to admit it was a fascinating mix.

Tory oversaw Cora as she brushed Star's strong body before tucking him into his stall. "Wonderful job as always, Cora. Pretty soon you won't need me to teach you a thing."

"That's so not true, Miss Tory." Cora slipped her hand in Tory's. They walked to the waiting car. "Someday I'll have a barn full of horses just like you."

"I don't doubt it." Tory waved until the car was out of view. She pressed her fists into the small of her back and stretched. Her dog Remi bumped her leg and leaned in offering the only comfort Tory would accept fully. "Hey girl." Soulful eyes sank into Tory's. "How's your day treating you?" Remi's gray streaked muzzle tipped up, tongue lolled. "Let's go check on Sweet Pea."

Tory walked through the barn and looked in on the laboring mare. The horse's agitation was obvious. She lifted her hind legs trying to kick her own belly. "Hurts, doesn't it?" Tory looked over the mare with experienced eyes. "I'd say you've shifted beyond pre-labor, honey." Sweet Pea ambled to the half door, pushed her nose against Tory's palm. "By tomorrow it will be over and you'll be a mommy. That will be worth it, don't you think?"

Her phone vibrated. Caution had Tory scanning the caller ID. Her brother's number lit the screen. Relief washed over her as she answered.

"Hey Aunt Tory, it's Riley."

"Who else would call me Aunt, squirt? Are you still my only nephew?"

"As far as I know, but I heard Mom and Dad talking in code. It's conceivable I might be up for a promotion. Get it Aunt Tory? Conceive-able."

"Subtle."

"These things happen, you realize."

The laid back acquiescence in his voice gave Tory's spirit a boost. Riley rambled in excited syllables about Lego Land and Space Mountain.

"…Dad nearly threw up, it was great. Mom is pulling the phone out of my hand. Gotta go."

Jess came on the line chuckling, "That boy, hi-ya Tory. How are you?"

"Good, fine…lonely."

"You should have come along. It truly is a magical place."

The women laughed and chatted. Tory spoke briefly to Murphy, filled him in on the rescue and updated him on ranch business. He sounded so relaxed and happy.

It made Tory think she should plan a vacation of her own. She lifted the bridle and saddle and placed them in their designated positions in the tack room.

"Ha," Tory poked fun at herself. "Exhaustion is making me delusional. A trip, a holiday…" Those words were a foreign language. "Oh, but I'm tired." The day had caught her. "I'll sit for a minute." Her knees softened and she lowered to the floor. "Two minutes."

Avery lifted the file Doc Webb had given him from the seat of his truck. He'd seen Tory dismiss the little girl at the conclusion of her lesson, and was certain she had ducked into the barn. He poked his head into stall after stall, but there was no sign of her. An odd noise met his ears as he approached the tack room. Avery stepped into the room of leather and brass and viewed multiple saddles arranged by size and style. Tidy to a fault, the ruthless organization spoke volumes to the heed and commitment of Keen Ranch.

The sound, soft and breathless, drew him deeper into the room.

She looked like a marionette whose strings had been snipped. Endless inches of leg were bent beneath her. Arms draped over her belly and thighs. Her head lolled forward and angled to one side. The banded tail of red hair draped over her shoulder. Her face was radiant even at rest. The rise and fall of her chest accompanied the whistle of breath passing her slightly parted lips.

Avery leaned against the support beam and appreciated the view.

She was a total contradiction. Her reputation had led him to expect conceit. Her fierce independence suggested arrogance but now that he'd witnessed her ease and dedication to animals, not to mention the gentle nature she showed with her student… There was a great deal more than he'd expected when it came to Tory Keen.

Silently he eased from the room.

—⁓—

Tory surged to her feet. Her hand flew to her hip when her phone pulsed. Heart racing, she flipped open the device, "What?"

"What's on second? Who's on first?" Her best friend Maggie's laughter trilled in her ear.

Tory shook the sleep from her head. "I just woke up in the barn."

"Juicy," Maggie drawled. "I hope you're not alone."

"Remind me why we are friends."

"Ooo…cranky, you're definitely alone. I'll give you a pass, since I know your day began at midnight."

"That's the horrible truth."

"I heard the police were onsite at the rescue," Maggie said. "Any new hotties?"

"No."

"You have permanent blinders," Maggie snickered. "Toned bodies wrapped in starched uniforms, holstered weapons, and handcuffs. Yum Yum."

"You're incorrigible."

"I am," Maggie laughed again. "Have to keep my dance card full."

Tory had no time for mingling with the opposite sex. Maggie on the other hand was a serial dater. Her latest fixation was cyber matchmaking. She'd gone global expanding her love of flirting to online dating sites. Maggie had threatened for weeks to drag Tory grudgingly into the electronic world of socialization. Tory yawned, "What time is it?"

"Dinner time. Ginny will be sending the search party if you don't find your way to the kitchen."

"But we had plans, didn't we?" Tory strolled from the barn.

"You get a pass on tonight too. Not a pass, a rain check," Maggie amended. "I'm creating your online dating profile with or without your consent."

"Without." Tory pushed open the mudroom door. Ginny was in the rocking chair asleep with her knitting. "Hanging up now, Maggie," she whispered. "Chat at you later."

Ginny gave the chair a gentle push. "I'm awake," she said without opening her eyes.

Tory walked to her side, kneeled. "It's been a long day for all of us. You should go home."

"I will as soon as you get your messages." Ginny motioned to the bar. "While you were with Cora, you had a call from the Equine Advocates. They want you to come and promote for funds at the fair. Point for me," Ginny continued over Tory's growl. "Doc Webb's delicious intern delivered the report from the rescue for your signature."

"Really, Ginny," Tory's eyes rolled.

"I'm no Mrs. Robinson, but I'm not dead." She handed Tory the file. "The goats made it through surgery and they've been upgraded to stable condition." Ginny stuffed her yarn and needles into her bag. "And in conclusion, that girlfriend of yours…"

"Is insane," Tory supplied.

"Extraordinarily enthusiastic for sure, but good-hearted, our Maggie." Ginny chuckled and levered her body from the chair. "Your dinner is on a plate in the oven, fruit salad in the fridge. I know you're tired but eat."

"I will," Tory lifted Ginny's coat from the rack and held it open. "Thank you."

"You are welcome." Ginny laid her wrinkled hand on Tory's cheek. "Rest."

CHAPTER SIX

Tory crawled from her bed while the sun slept on. The dogs shifted and consumed the vacated spot. She maneuvered through the dark to the bathroom while loosening the knots in her hair. She scrubbed the sleep from her eyes, toned and moisturized her skin, brushed and flossed her teeth. Hygiene regimen complete, Tory pulled on her thermal shirt and jeans and fashioned a rope braid to contain her strands.

From the top of the stairs she could hear Ginny in the kitchen. Her voice, a faint whisper, joined a ballad from *Les Misérables*. Tory restrained the bladder motivated dogs. If she was lucky Ginny would lose herself in the tasks of meal prep and sing a full verse before buttoning her lips.

Her day was off to a fortunate start.

She released her grasp on the dogs' collars, followed their rush of energy down the steps.

Tory shoved the galley door aside and inhaled. Crisp turkey bacon sizzled on the griddle beside perfectly bronzed French toast. Another pan was mounded with chunks of seasoned potatoes. Tory's mouth watered. She had always enjoyed a healthy appetite. Lucky for her the physical labor ranching required allowed her the extra calories.

"Morning, Tory love," Ginny hummed another bar. "You ever come to my kitchen late I'll know you've been up to no good."

"How could I ever be late to a breakfast this fine?" Tory hitched her hip on a stool as Ginny placed a luscious pink grapefruit, sliced, sectioned, and sugared in front of her.

"Talk about fine," Ginny lowered the heat on the potatoes. "Doc Webb has his sexy shadow with him this morning."

Tory quirked her brow, "He's early." She started to push away from the bar.

"Sit," Ginny said simply. "You'll eat, you'll go put a little female business on your face and you'll choose a nicer shirt, before you head out to the barn."

"Female business?"

"Some color, blusher, mascara, and pink up your lips while you're at it."

"I'll do no such thing." Tory speared a bite of French toast, "I'm spending the day in the barn."

Ginny looked down her nose and shook her head. "Manners, Tory love." She wiped her hands on her apron, and slid the morning paper across the counter.

The front page headline and photo showed Tory leading the abused mare to the trailer. More images captured Doc Webb with his arms wrapped protectively around one of the goats. There also was a quote in bold print from the man responsible for the horror.

"You are spoiling my breakfast." Tory flipped the paper over and loaded her fork. "Your cooking? That's news. But I'd rather keep your talents undiscovered and your body tied to the stove at the Keen Ranch." Tory savored the next bite.

Ginny piled a plate with French toast and bacon and climbed on the stool next to Tory. "I do my best."

"You ever going to tell me your secret?" Tory teased.

"If I tell you my secret, you'll have no reason to keep me around."

"That is not true."

"Mmm, milk, eggs, vanilla, and…something else…"

"Yeah, the secret part."

The rap of nail guns announced the arrival of the construction crew. Tory's eyes tracked to the heavy sheet of plastic which separated the dirt of the cottage rehab from Ginny's pristine kitchen.

"So my darling girl, how is your little summerhouse project coming?" Ginny had been peeking at the progress every day from the kitchen window. She preferred to ask Tory so she could hear the excitement straight from Tory's lips.

"The contractor assured me he'd finish the interior today. The plumber promised the bath renovation would be done tomorrow, so in the spirit of positive thinking, I hope to get painting in the next day or two."

"It's going to be a cozy little spot for you."

"Why did Murphy have to fall in love and upset my simple life?" There was no heat in her words.

"You can't hide your happiness from me, Tory love." Ginny patted her arm, "and I'm neck deep in it with you." The mudroom door opened.

"Knock, knock," Maggie shouted over the commotion of the dogs scurrying in ahead of her.

Ginny touched Maggie's twin pigtails. "Good morning, little girl."

Maggie plopped her tote on the floor then placed a basket of delectable baked goods on the counter.

"I thought I was coming to your house tonight," Tory asked.

"You are, but I made a few extra pastries, thought your hammer swinging hunks might appreciate a treat."

"Which one," Tory heaved a resigned sigh.

"I haven't a clue what you are talking about." Maggie's lashes fluttered innocently then she lifted her palm in carefree submission. "I've got my eye on the lean hunk with the bulging biceps, and thick curly black hair." She leaned close to the window.

Ginny and Tory squeezed on either side, angling for a look at the man in question.

"Married," Tory said flatly.

"Killjoy." Maggie leaned closer, "He's new. Yum Yum."

Tory nudged her aside and studied the silhouette. Feet braced wide, hands on narrow hips. "Don't know that one. Another day, another carpenter."

"I'll start with him." Maggie lifted her hood leaving her pigtails dangling at her collarbone. "Who can resist me?" She scooped up her basket of muffins and a fistful of napkins. "I'm Little Red Riding Hood."

Tory snickered, "Inviting all the wolves to taste your treats."

"That was good!" Maggie's laughter filled the kitchen. "Whatever you put in her breakfast, Ginny, well done. Excuse me, time to ogle hard-bodies. See you later, Tory, unless I get gobbled up."

Knuckles rapped lightly on the back door. Boot clad feet stomped off dirt on the thick mat. "Anyone up?" Dale called.

"It's daylight, isn't it?" Ginny quipped. "Doc Webb with you?"

"Yep." Dale and Doc Webb tossed their coats on the pegs by the door and walked into the kitchen.

"Morning, ladies," Doc Webb moved comfortably to the steaming pot of coffee. He brought them up to speed on the goats' surgery. "I checked Ariel, lookin' like she is settling in." He sipped the strong coffee. "Sweet Pea dropped a healthy filly overnight. The rest of the expectant mares are all healthy. Probably have a few deliver in the next two weeks. Rest should hold 'til I get home."

Tory sulked.

Ginny rested her hand on Doc Webb's shoulder. "What a lovely way to celebrate all those years of marriage. I'll expect you and the Mrs. for dinner after so I can look at hundreds of photos. I want to hear a firsthand accounting of each ray of sun, taste of wine, and morsel of food." Ginny kissed his cheek, "Happy Anniversary."

"Yes, yes, congratulations," Tory's enthusiasm barely marked the Richter scale. "I don't mean to be selfish, but who am I calling if my mares decide to drop at the same time?"

"What am I, some upstart?" Dale cocked a hip. He'd been working the ranch as long as Ginny had tended the stove.

"You know what I mean, what if we hit trouble?" Tory implored Doc Webb.

"You hit anything you can't handle, call Avery. I brought him along today to see the layout, get familiar."

"The shadow," Ginny winked at Tory.

"The shadow?" Dale looked confused.

Doc Webb dipped his hand into his back pocket and passed Tory a business card. "He is staying in the apartment at my place. House number, pager, personal cell, you probably won't even need to call."

"You know if you bring strays inside and feed them they never leave."

"Here's hoping." Doc Webb clinked his mug to hers. His eyes twinkled with mischief. "He's the one." He tapped his finger on the card Tory had laid on the counter. "He's knowledgeable, focused, an all around great guy."

"I'll be right out to meet him."

"He's gone," Doc Webb sipped his coffee.

Tory frowned, "You've met him, Dale?"

"I have. Solid and eager."

"Advertisement for a high-quality hunting dog," She muttered and carried her plate to the sink. "You're certain?" She searched Doc Webb's face for any signs of doubt. He nodded firmly. Tory raised a shoulder and slipped the card into her hip pocket. "Then that will have to do."

Doc Webb offered Tory a thick folder. "Sorry you'll have to cover the hearing solo."

"Wednesday, 11:00 AM."

"Gives you a week to get everything in order. I'll need you to look over Avery's written assessment of the goats and of course do a final evaluation on Ariel."

"No problem." Tory patted the folder. "I'll do you proud."

"Don't I know it." The men topped off their coffee and vanished to the stables. Ginny untied and folded her apron. "What's your day lookin' like?"

"I need to make a trip into town." Tory groaned, "Shopping."

"Internet is the only way. What's on your list?"

"I need presentable clothes for the hearing, and a haircut. I also want to pick up some items for the cottage, and Riley's birthday is coming fast. Better if I see things in person."

"You'll be gone all day. You want company, or can I jot some things on your list and add to your burden?"

Tory smiled. Ginny hated shopping nearly as much as she did. "Thanks for offering to come along, but you hold down the fort. I'm planning to swing by Maggie's on the way home."

"Signing you up for Barnyard Bachelors," she snickered.

"The price I'll pay to sweet talk her into helping me paint this weekend."

"She'll do it if you asked," Ginny said simply.

"But then I'll owe her. If it's her idea…"

"Smart girl."

The phone rang. Tory scowled.

"Don't fuss." Ginny wiped her hands on her apron. "I have a wager to win." She patted Tory's arm in comfort, lifted the receiver. "Miss Keen is occupied at the moment, but I'd be happy to help you." Tory drove the remaining bites of food around her plate and listened to Ginny relay the Keen Ranch web address.

"Well?"

Ginny replaced the receiver and made a notation on the message pad. "Donation, one hundred dollars."

"Good." Tory walked to the sink and rinsed her plate. "Doc Webb's bill for fixing those goats is going to be substantial." Tory soaped the dishcloth and rubbed the counter and the bar. "What do you get if you win?"

"Me?" Ginny smiled, "I get a trip to the fair and twenty dollars for food."

"And Dale?"

"Homemade pie."

"For what it's worth I hope you'll be baking pie, I hate personal events and begging for money."

"I know you do," Ginny pacified. "But those photos you displayed of Star after you rescued him tripled the donations last year."

Tory wrinkled her nose.

Ginny pressed now, "You remember his condition."

Tory would never forget. His ribs were so protruded every single one was visible.

"And this year you have countless photos of Cora grooming and riding him. He looks like a champion."

"I know you're right," Tory mumbled.

"Star is the best example of what you are able to do for the rescues." Ginny rubbed Tory's shoulder.

"Maybe I should take Cora to the fair…little girl, adorable riding outfit, ribboned pigtails. People will trip over themselves to donate."

"Like I said," Ginny chuckled. "You're a very smart girl."

CHAPTER SEVEN

Avery pinned the cell phone between his ear and shoulder as he fished his credit card out of his wallet. The voice on the other end of the line grew more persistent with every sentence. "I'd be pleased to arrange travel and hotel for you. Springtime on the Eastern Shore is quite beautiful."

"I'm sure it is," Avery smiled at the cashier and signed the slip. "However, I'm committed for the next two weeks." He moved away from the counter while the clerk bagged his merchandise. The orthopedic practice was pursuing him like a relentless Jack Russell. "I'm happy to fly to Maryland, as previously discussed, when the obligations of my internship are fulfilled."

"Two weeks," the voice confirmed. "It will be such a pleasure to meet you in person. In the meantime we have secured your educational sessions in Denver."

Avery bit back a growl. He'd forgotten about the veterinary conference. "I'm not sure I can…"

"Certainly the Midwestern practice can spare an intern for two days. It's a quick trip and an overnight." Her unappreciative tone shut off any further protest. "I will email the travel confirmation within the hour."

Avery exited the building and leaned against the bricks of the shopping center. Doc Webb wouldn't be thrilled about an overnight absence, but he'd understand. He may not have formally offered Avery a permanent position, but his intentions were apparent.

Doc Webb, a patient, persistent coonhound to rival the terrier.

The clouds were shifting from winter white to smoky gray. "Better get the fashion in the car." Avery slung the suit over his shoulder and headed for his truck.

The trip had taken twice as long as she'd expected.

The salon visit proved a grave miscalculation. The hot topic of the day turned out to be the rescue. Tory, the wet headed captive of the hydraulic chair, endured relentless questioning from the salon staff and patrons.

A colossal migraine had taken root before she was blown dry.

Laden with a myriad of bags, Tory crossed the endless sea of pavement. "Hate shopping. Hate, hate, hate, shopping."

Fat drops of rain began to fall from the sky. Tory huffed. Seasons changed in the Midwest like the mind of a pubescent female, without warning or sensibility.

Grateful for wet not white, she reached into her satchel, and fished for her keys.

The rain fell faster plastering her freshly coiffed hair to her neck and shoulders. "Terrific." Tory juggled her purchases and performed a full body search. With a snarl she crouched down to rummage in her bag.

The rain abruptly stopped rebounding off her scalp. She twisted and glanced through drenched tresses into a striking face sheltered beneath an enormous blue and white striped umbrella.

"No use getting soaked while you locate your keys," his voice rumbled.

"Um...ahh," Tory's mouth dropped open.

"You leave anything in the store?" He motioned toward the merchandise spilling over the pavement.

"Renovation, housewarming, birthday party – a first, he's nine." Her brain muddled as his brows lowered and framed potent blue eyes.

"A first birthday but he's nine? Should I call Ripley's?"

"My nephew, newly acquired. His mother married my brother, modern family. This is his first birthday celebration with me."

He nodded at her pile. "I think you may have overdone it."

She looked at the bags, "You may be right. Maybe I should save some for Christmas. Found 'em." Tory jingled her key ring, then unlocked the hatch.

He lifted a bag loaded with gingham checked tea towels, oven mitts, coordinated placemats, and matching salt, pepper, and sugar containers.

"The kitchen store," Tory explained. "Huge sale, I got carried away."

"It's been known to happen." The ridiculously handsome stranger continued to frown at her. He gathered an errant shoebox, "And shoes."

Tory laughed nervously. "A weakness, but what woman can resist shoes?" The intensity of his gaze sparked unease, the sort welcomed by her twenty-seven-year-old libido. Tory studied his profile. There was something familiar about him. "Have we met?"

"I've been out to your ranch." He closed the hatch.

She snapped her fingers, "The carpenter."

His wide palm pressed against her low back, as he ushered her to the driver's door. Flustered at the chivalrous gesture, Tory slid behind the wheel. "Who says all the good men are in Alaska?"

"What?"

Gracious, had she said that out loud? "An article I read," Tory waved, dismissing the comment. "Thanks for the shelter."

"Not a problem. Drive safely, Miss Keen."

The door snapped shut. Tory studied his face through the streaked window. Her breath fogged the cold pane of glass. Drawn to speak with him, or at the very least ask his name, she fumbled for the door handle. She glanced down, grasped the lever and looked up in time to see his figure disappearing into the rain.

She turned the engine over and flipped the heater on full. "Too cold in Alaska." Tory squeezed the precipitation from her hair, "Even if men outnumber women seven to one."

CHAPTER EIGHT

The car bumped along the narrow dirt lane leading to Maggie's small log, two-bedroom home. Once a general store, Maggie had converted the open floor plan into a family room and catering kitchen. She worked constantly filling orders for her online business which offered decorative cookies and baked goods, and a variety of signature salsas. Tory tried not to visit in the evening because without doubt Maggie would pull something sinful from the oven and they'd sample until they were sick.

Tory eased from the car, tensed when she spotted Maggie's apron. She prayed to the gods of favorable calories Maggie wasn't making pastry. Salsa she could justify, but Maggie's baked goods were another story. "What's cooking?"

"I know if I say salsa you'll stay and visit, but I'm not going to lie to you." Maggie's head tipped to the side, "Cake."

Tory groaned.

"A specialty cake," Maggie rushed on. "It's the first one I've tried and I actually could use your opinion if you wouldn't mind. Not a tasting, 'cause I know I'm good." Maggie snapped her fingers then propped her hand on her hip. "I just need you to look at it."

Intrigued Tory closed the car door. "All right, I'm curious."

"Love the haircut. Sexy layers, all slick, straight, and shiny. I'd kill for your hair."

"There are days I'd give it to you."

"So the cake… just come in and take a look. The client made a special request. I'll know if I've got it right if you can tell what it is." Maggie nibbled nervously on her thumbnail. She led Tory into the kitchen stopping beside the wide counter. "Come around to this side so it's not upside down. There now, look."

Tory studied the cake. It looked like… Tory cocked her head to the side. Long, rounded at the top and sort of had two spheres at the bottom. "It looks like a…I don't want to say it, especially if I'm wrong. Is it a… well, it reminds me of a…"

Maggie's cheeks were bright pink, "A penis?"

"I didn't want to guess that." Tory laughed. "A penis, really? Who would want such a thing?"

"Bachelorette party," Maggie lifted her hands. "One of my longest running clients ordered it. She loves my cakes and asked if I'd do a wiener for her best friend's bachelorette party. I told her I needed to experiment before I agreed to the contract." Maggie shrugged. "If you think it looks like a…you know…I guess I'm in the right ball park."

Tory snorted. "I'd say you are in the *ball*-park." She laughed heartily. "Never can predict what people will ask for in a creative business." Unable to resist, Tory swiped her index finger along the icing. "You know I have zero willpower." The digit disappeared into her mouth. The moan that followed was lustful. "I hate you."

"No, you don't." Maggie grinned. "Give it a moment. Let the sugar seep in." Her nerves had passed. "What have you been doing, besides sneaking spa time? You look tired, and wet."

"A haircut is hardly a trip to the spa." Tory rolled her eyes. "Shopping."

Maggie sympathized with her best friend's disdain for retail adventures, although she didn't agree with it. "What would make you do that?" Maggie grabbed two plates from the cupboard.

"I have to present at the abuse hearing next week."

"Right, Doc Webb is taking his wife away." She sighed, "Forty years… to have and to hold. It's the sweetest."

"So everyone keeps saying." Tory rolled her eyes. "I hit the Emporium of Bath and Bed, plus grabbed some paint samples and bought Riley's birthday gift. I was informed I went overboard."

"Bought too much? That's an odd thing for a sales clerk to point out." Maggie sliced off a sliver of cake and laid it on the plate.

Tory scowled at the dish. "Not a clerk. A brooding, blue eyed, umbrella wielding, hunk of man."

40

"Oooo, shopping had perks." Maggie moved around the bar, grabbed napkins and utensils. "Do tell."

"It's nothing. He provided shelter from the rain while I loaded the obscene amount of products I'd accumulated in ninety minutes."

"You do it well when your hand is forced." Maggie chuckled. "Who was he, this gallant Adonis?"

Tory wagged her fork at her grinning friend. "Every moment is not a romantic rendezvous."

"It could be. I should be out with a dreamy man sipping champagne and nibbling on chocolates, but tonight my hot date is an oven set at 350 degrees."

Tory chuckled.

"Continue, the hunk of man?"

"A carpenter from the springhouse crew, I didn't get his name."

Maggie hummed, "Intrigue…suspense."

"Your pursuit of happily-ever-after runs as hot as your oven."

"Hotter." Maggie filled two glasses with freshly brewed tea. "Honey? Lemon?"

Tory nodded. She didn't share Maggie's enthusiasm for relationships. In her mind, affairs of the heart were as unpredictable and inaccurately predicted as the changing atmosphere. Tory's fork stopped a fraction from her lips. "You gave me cake."

"I gave you X-rated cake, that's what best friends do for one another," Maggie said wistfully as she set the lemon wedges and honey jar between them. "You think I'd be tired of eating my brilliance." She tasted her dessert and savored, "But I'm not. They met online, you know. The penis cake couple."

"Not safe to put all your personal business on the internet." Tory added a heaping spoonful of honey to her tea.

"Safe as chapel," Maggie insisted. "I enjoy cyber chatting. No strings, no pressure, you will too. I signed you up."

Tory jolted. "You what!"

"I told you I was going to." Maggie tapped a few keys on her laptop then spun it towards Tory. "Here's your profile. Lookie here, you have a wink and a poke already."

"I have no idea what that means. More importantly, I don't care." Tory lifted her mug and sipped. "Who has time to sift through profiles? Let alone to exert the effort required to maintain a healthy relationship?"

The computer chirped. "Awesome, another wink! You're on your way to a hot date and steamy sex."

"I have no need for steamy sex."

"Don't be foolish." Maggie waved her hand dismissing Tory. "It's been forever since…"

"Maggie."

"What? It's the truth." She tapped a few keys. "Here's your wink-man's profile. Bradley Charles. He's a breeder. Well, that sounded bad. He's in the horse business." Maggie nodded, "A common thread. Fifty-two. Divorced, with six children."

"Six!" Tory squeaked. "For the love of…" she rested her head on the counter.

"Kidding, I set your age range preference from twenty-one to forty-five."

"Twenty-one!"

"Cougar." Maggie's laughter was so rich and contagious Tory couldn't help but join in. "My point, dear friend, it's been too long since either of us has had anyone worthy of fresh sheets and body oil."

"I'll settle for kind, considerate, and clean."

"Yes, blood tests nowadays are an important step."

Tory moaned, "T-M-I."

"T-M-I is the order I placed for a multi speed, dual-action, waterproof, hide in the bedside table buddy."

"Nasty." Tory shook her head and sipped.

"You say that now," Maggie giggled, "but in ten to fourteen days you'll adore this particular brand of nasty. They were having a buy-one-get-one sale. We need to stock up on AA batteries."

Tory sputtered and grasped her napkin.

"But in the meantime," Maggie sipped. "Let's take a closer look at Bradley Charles, the breeder."

"Let's not." Tory savored the final morsel of cake and resisted the urge to tap her finger across the empty pottery to collect the crumbs.

Maggie powered off the computer, lifted their plates, carried them to the sink. "Let's transition to a more agreeable subject. "How's your cottage?"

"Amazing, Joel's design is just," Tory hummed, "as great as your cake."

Maggie flinched. She'd had a crush on Tory's honorary brother from the moment they'd pedaled bikes on the dirt surrounding Keen Ranch. He'd stolen a kiss the summer she'd turned sixteen, stolen more when she'd turned eighteen. The memory heated her cheeks. Delectable, spectacular, just-like-Joel, cake… tasty, Maggie thought, and started to clean up the kitchen.

"Why don't you chat with Joel? He's safe."

Maggie dropped her mixing bowl. Stainless met porcelain with a clatter. Joel was not safe by Maggie's estimation. She flipped on the tap and filled the bowl with sudsy water.

Tory moved to her side. "He crosses the Mississippi four times a year."

"Seems more often than that," Maggie muttered. "The online men I chat with are phantoms. No risk of them popping up in my real world. Joel is real."

"You're damn right he is."

"Enough," Maggie dried her hands and folded the towel over the rack. "I don't want to discuss Joel. Let's go back a beat. When do I get my tour of your cottage? I know you're dying to rub your premium appliances in my face." She ripped off a piece of saran wrap to cover the extra icing.

"They are not suitable for your type of work."

"I promise I can take it." She smiled with more sweetness than her famous frosting.

"Stop over tomorrow night. You can look at my paint swatches and help me visualize furniture placement. The work is pretty much done inside. The contractor needs to finish the spouting on the breezeway." Tory carried the bowl and set it in the refrigerator. "It's time for paint, paper, furniture, and…"

Maggie bounced on her toes. "I want to paint."

"Sick."

"I'll pack a bag and stay for the whole weekend. We'll cover walls in color until we drop, then wake up and do it all over again. Maggie clapped. "Slumber party! I'm so excited."

"Only you would applaud a forty-eight hour home improvement session."

"I love, love, love," she twirled her apron flying like a five-year-old's tutu, "to paint."

"You may paint anything you want." Tory laughed at her friend.

"Let me do all the trim. It's so meticulous like icing a cake."

"I gain weight just listening to you," Tory groaned.

CHAPTER NINE

Tory high fived and hugged. It was a ruckus afternoon dismissal, but exactly what you would expect from teenagers. Every Friday since the group had been in sixth grade the kids offered their youthful energy to the Keen Ranch, mucking stalls, tending the foals, and nurturing the rescues. What had begun as a junior high project had become a spark of passion. Graduation was a few months away. Tory was thrilled to learn each was pursuing a career linked to the ranching industry.

The horizon had begun to lure the sun. Tinges of orange and red were beginning to smudge the blue canvas. It was Tory's turn to finish early. She always felt guilty quitting before the sun but rotating the late nights assured proper rest for everyone who worked on the ranch.

She strolled toward the stables. Dale was grooming Peach, her brother's prize. A gorgeous chestnut mare, Peach was seven months into an eleven-month pregnancy. Bred to a champion stallion, the foal she carried would increase the quality of the Keen Ranch's line of horses.

"She's looking good."

"A stunner for sure," he ran a soft brush across Peach's flank. "Thought I'd walk her a bit before I turn her out for recess."

"Perfect," Tory ran her hand over Peach's nose. "I need to call Murphy and tell him how beautiful you are." The mare nudged Tory's hip looking for a treat. Tory dipped her hands into her pocket and produced a small white cube of sugar.

Dale clucked his tongue. "Spoiling her."

"Yes, I am," Tory rubbed Peach's strong neck. "She won't tattle on me."

"Neither will I," Dale smiled. "You finished up?"

"I'll feed the rescues before I call it a day."

"Bet you'd rather tend livestock all weekend than slap paint on those primed walls of yours."

"You would be right."

"You and Maggie mind your footing on the ladders." He hooked a lead to Peach's halter. "Let's go burn off that sugar."

Tory pushed the farm cart burdened with bales of hay toward the rescue corral. Smooch rushed to the fence. "If only you had a big fluffy tail to wag." She laughed and crossed to his enclosure. He angled his head through the fencing and pressed his lips to hers. The horses whinnied at the delay in their dinner service. Tory distributed chunks to all the rescues then tossed a wedge of hay to Ariel.

Two days had done wonders for her condition. The visible improvements to her coat were a direct reflection of proper nutrition and hygiene. The wound on her leg had begun to heal. Forty-eight hours had produced other progress on the ranch. Three new foals had entered the world without incident. Birthing, nature's wildcard, was a delight when it went well. With Doc Webb out of town Tory hoped the blissful streak would continue.

Elton John's *Avita* greeted Tory as she walked into the warmth of the house. She stepped out of her boots and hooked her coat and hat on the pegs in the mudroom.

The sauté pan sizzled. The fragrance exploded and filled the room. Ginny diced onion, garlic, and a horde of herbs and spices. "I'm putting together a hearty lasagna for dinner." Ginny lined up the ingredients on the counter top like school children.

Tory tried to retain the order in which the magic happened. Dazzled and intoxicated by the organic choreography she gave up. Ginny's secret would remain secure.

Ginny covered the layered casserole with a sheet of foil and untied her apron. "I walked through your cottage today." She placed two mugs on the counter and filled the steeping spoon with tea leaves. "It looks so big."

"That's because it's empty."

"Not for long," Ginny lifted the kettle and poured the water. "When is Maggie invading?"

"Any moment." Tory wrapped her fingers around the mug and lifted it to her nose.

"I'm sure she'll bring treats. Get you all hopped up on sugar and worse."

Tory laughed, "Hopped up?"

"Cranked, amped, toasted, baked." Ginny swatted Tory's hip with the tea towel. "I watch reality television and read your Cosmo magazines."

"Tremendous source of information," Tory stated.

"Agreed, especially the sex advice," she winked. "Not in the grave yet." The dogs barked and rushed to the door. "I made plenty of dinner. Feed her. All the girl eats is pastry."

"Hey ladies," Maggie burst into the room in sweatpants streaked with remnants of previous painting projects.

"Dressed for the job."

"Of course," Maggie unzipped her tote and wagged an unopened bottle of vodka at Tory. "Hooray for painting! Juice and snacks are in the car. Back in a jiffy."

"You two will be in trouble before you lift a brush." Ginny shifted the liquor off her counter. "End up running the roller crooked."

"Maybe that will make it fun," Tory said dryly.

Ginny tipped her head low, leveled her gaze with Tory's. "Be certain to eat as well as drink."

"Yes, ma'am."

"And stow the leftovers in the refrigerator."

"You should sleep in tomorrow. In fact, take the weekend off. Maggie and I are going to roll on through until Sunday."

"I will take that offer. I'm in the middle of Season Two of *Downton Abbey*. The war is raging and the girls are getting into all kinds of delicious tangles with inappropriate men."

Nerves bubbled as Tory led her friend into the summer house. "Keep in mind this is a work in progress."

"Shhh," Maggie stood in the living room and pivoted slowly as if riding a lazy susan. When her circle completed, her smile radiated pure joy. "This is your home," she said reverently.

Tory grinned at her friend, "It's going to be perfect, right?"

"Lead on."

The women followed the narrow hall. A split staircase led up to a small office and walk-in closet, and down to a bedroom. A pocket door maximized the space and concealed an indulgent full bath with a multi-head shower stall and pedestal sink.

Maggie traced her finger over the brushed brass faucet. "Everything is larger than it seems."

"It's the layout. Not sure how Joel did it." Tory gestured broadly to the room.

"Purple," Maggie stated.

"What?"

"Like the illusion of color with fashion. You dress a woman in black, she looks small, slender. But purple..." Maggie shuddered, "Doesn't matter the size, that's a whole lot of color."

Tory snickered at Maggie's logic. "He made my summer house fat?"

"The f-word is unkind. Joel made your cottage purple."

Tory pulled a folder from a drawer. "I used these for my inspiration."

Maggie flipped through the collages. Tory had jotted notes in the margins along with dimensions and estimated prices. "It's like furnishing a doll house."

"I made newspaper templates." Tory spread the stencils across the island. The small space in her cottage could be maximized with the right chair and side table.

"Did you order all this?"

"Dreaming and drooling over the leather loveseat. Most of the pieces are recycles and I will be pulling a few from the main house."

"What about this hutch? Reproduction?"

"If it has to be," Tory laid the huge section of paper on the floor beside the door leading to the breezeway. "I found one I like online, but it's a gamble to purchase an antique without seeing it in person."

"True."

"Joel offered to build one for me."

"What can't that man do?"

"I know it." Tory pointed to the counter, "Grab the paper marked love seat, I'll get the coffee table. We'll shift them and decide which fits the best."

CHAPTER TEN

Tory had hoped to finish her neglected paperwork but she wakened at 8:45 PM drooling on the desk. She turned out the lights, walked from the barn to the empty house.

The epic weekend of paint had rolled into a sequel of vacuum cleaners, scrub buckets, paper towels and glass cleaner. She ached in places she hadn't known existed. Even the follicles on her head were exhausted. Another day, maybe two, to move furnishings then she'd be ready to relocate her clothing and officially spend the night in her cottage home.

She stripped while climbing the stairs and navigated the dark hall to her room. In a few hours Monday, most dreaded of days, would lead the charge into her week. A week which would include the animal cruelty hearing, the veterinary convention, and her brother's homecoming. "Tranquilize me now."

She fell onto her bed with a graceless plop, nestled beneath the covers and surrendered to sleep.

Avery had survived forty-eight hours at the helm of Doc Webb's veterinary practice. Barely.

The first day, he had been called to a ranch where a horse was refusing to care for her newborn foal. He had bottled fed abandoned kittens as a teenager, so he reasoned his way into loading the orphaned black colt into his truck, taking him to the clinic.

Twelve hours later, humbled to the point of collapse, Avery learned tending a newborn horse was by no means the same undertaking as kittens in a cardboard box. He called for backup. Doc

Webb's loyal student brigade divided the demanding schedule, and thanked him for sharing the experience.

Day two passed with routine office visits and a neutering. Avery powered down the computer and strolled through the clinic to check on his patients one final time before locking up.

A girl pushed through the door with textbooks burdening her arms, and a pink bubble expanding from her lips. Topping her stack of coveted knowledge was a thirty-two ounce energy drink. "I'm on the phones until seven AM. What's the status of the souls in the back?"

"The colt is doing better every minute, the goats are getting stronger, and Charlie, a retriever, who as of two o'clock forfeited his right to father pups, is resting comfortably. Everyone is tucked in for the night."

"Excellent," she snapped her gum. "Fingers crossed for a quiet night. Huge exam next week."

Avery drove to his apartment. The mountains, a shadow stone boundary, punctuated his vision. A single gleaming star and moonbeams were the only light across the untarnished acres. He savored the silence and the dark.

He set the pager on the bedside table. He stripped his shirt over his head and fell onto the spacious bed and wished for a peaceful night.

Tory bolted to ninety degrees. Reflex had her scooping the phone up. "Yes, what? I'm here." The red digits on the clock read ten minutes till twelve.

"It's Dale. We've a problem with Peach."

Feet in socks, legs in jeans, Tory buttoned and zipped. "She's not due for months." She pulled her sweatshirt over her head, headed to the stairs.

"Tell her that."

"On my way."

Dale met Tory at the stable door and heaved it closed against the cold night behind her. "She's fighting because she knows it's too early. But something else is up, heart rate is too high."

"Her water break?"

"No."

"Good, we've got time." Equine birth typically required little or no human interaction. The process of delivery, fairly quick, would be complete thirty minutes after the mare's water broke.

Tory hurried to Peach's stall then deliberately slowed and took a deep breath. It wouldn't do any good to transfer her angst to the troubled mare.

She looked over the stall's half door. "Oh Dale," she whispered. Peach lay on her side. Sweat dampened her neck. Her eyes glazed with pain and panic. Tory faced Dale, "Call Doc Webb."

"He's gone, left for his trip."

Tory grimaced and pulled her cell phone from her hip pocket and cued up the contact information Doc Webb had given her for the stand-in. She punched the numbers, huffed when the afterhour's voicemail kicked on. Tory disconnected and dialed the scrawled cell phone number written on the back.

A gruff voice came on the line, "Hello."

"I'm trying to reach Avery Rush, the veterinarian covering for Doc Webb."

"You got him."

"This is Tory Keen. I've got a mare delivering early. She's having a lot of trouble."

"Is Dale on? Perhaps he could run the details with me."

Tory bit down on her annoyance. "Yes, Dale is here, but I'm the one calling."

Avery cleared his throat. "The emergency fee is $2,500."

"I don't give two shakes about your billable rate, Dr. Rush. Doc Webb said you were the man to call."

"I'm just trying to be certain you need me to come out."

"You want my damn Visa number?" Her irritation neared anger.

"Be there in fifteen minutes."

The gruff string of words Tory mumbled when she disconnected warned Dale not to ask questions.

"I hope Doc Webb's wonder boy has a better bedside manner with horses than humans."

CHAPTER ELEVEN

Tory gripped the latch, rotated the metal, and opened the pen. A soft murmur of incoherent syllables matched her movement like music as she joined the mare. Tory rubbed her hands briskly to gather warmth and knelt in the soft straw. She rested her palms behind Peach's ears, then slid them slowly over her head and neck hitting pressure points to aid in relaxation.

Dale looked on as Tory transferred relief. He could have sworn Peach sighed. Her eyes lost the edge of fear as the degree of pain eased.

The seconds ticked like a tortoise moving through mud. Finally the stand-in vet entered the barn. Whatever Tory had expected, it wasn't the carpenter, slash umbrella wielding man, she had bumped into over the past several days. She staunched the desire to pepper him with questions, and demand proof of license.

He examined Peach's twelve-hundred pound form from neck to flank. Tory appreciated Avery's proficiency and calm manner. His confidence put her at ease and went a long way to eliminating her initial impression.

Avery's brow creased in concentration. "I can see why you are not pleased with this situation, Miss Peach." He stood, braced fists on hips, and tipped his head to heaven. His lips were drawn in a tight line when he faced Tory and Dale with a look of utter despair, "Twins."

Tory's breath whooshed out along with a razor-sharp vicious curse from Dale.

Not a blessing in the equine community. Dangerous to mother and foal, only one in ten thousand twin pregnancies progressed successfully to term. A mare was to be monitored after breeding to insure only a single embryo.

Dale scrubbed his hands over his face. "How could we have missed it?"

"No time to worry over that now." Tory prayed for a miracle and through unshed tears asked, "You're certain?" At Avery's curt nod, she stifled her emotions. "We need to do our best for Peach."

Peach whinnied softly as her water broke. She fought to keep pace with the mounting contractions.

Sweat beaded across Tory's forehead. Her exertion and focus intent on the ailing mare. Avery met each challenge with practiced patience. He had nerves of steel, while hers boiled beneath her skin. Not a single fleck of uncertainty. He assessed and calculated before making a decision.

Murmuring to himself, he manipulated the foals for easier passage. Perspiration coated his thermal shirt. Avery felt Tory's eyes scrutinizing his every move like a proctor monitoring a major exam. He wanted her to be impressed with his skill, but knew she watched for accountability.

She had surprised him. Even with Doc Webb's adulation, Avery had anticipated a little hesitation during the difficult delivery. But Tory had jumped in, and more. Her hands in constant contact with Peach were as successful as an injection of medication.

The promise of new life vanished when the stillborn twins were pulled from Peach's womb.

Dale wrapped the unmoving foals in a blanket. "I'll take care of them." His voice fractured with exhaustion and sadness. "You stay with Peach."

Hot tears streaked Tory's cheeks. "I'll help." She kissed Peach gently and shifted to follow Dale.

"If you wouldn't mind, Miss Keen, I'd like if you stayed with Peach." Avery said quietly. "Her job isn't over quite yet."

Tory wasn't a novice at participating in the birthing process. She nodded and soothed Peach as the contractions began for the delivery of the afterbirth. Tory ran the tips of her fingers over Peach's face. The mare's eyes appeared drenched in unwept tears.

Avery studied Tory. For as much as she had taken charge on the scene of the rescue, she followed his directions without question as he led Peach through the birth.

Peach lifted her head and with a majestic thrust of muscle, regained her feet.

"That's a good sign." Tory scurried out of her way.

Avery sealed the contents into a medical waste bag. "I can't stand losing foals." He stripped off his gloves and gathered the soiled towels. "Miss Keen?"

"Please, after what we've endured, call me Tory."

Avery cleared his throat. "Tory, I realize you and I had a poor start on our professional relationship, but I have a proposition for you."

"I'd say you have to be pretty hard up to proposition a woman who looks the way I do."

A ghost of a smile cracked through Avery's fatigue riddled face. "I have a situation that you and Peach could help me with." Avery pulled a bandana from his pocket and wiped the sweat from his face. "I've been tending an orphan, a colt. His mom refused him almost as soon as his hooves hit the straw. I have read articles about fostering using nurse mares."

"How old is your colt?" she interrupted. "Statistics of success are higher if he's close in age to the one we are replacing."

Avery smiled. Of course Tory would have an understanding of the process. "He was born two days ago. The clinic volunteers are tending him round the clock. Keeping him hydrated is a delicate mission."

Tory's grief laden brain switched modes. She leaned against the stall door and began to process the logistics of Avery's idea.

"I recognize it's an odd request." Avery rushed on. "I would like to see if Peach might accept the little guy as her own. A mother is more apt to receive a foal that isn't hers if…"

Lost in thought, Avery's voice fell distant and disconnected to Tory's ears. He stood directly in front of her. She shook her head clear and focused on his earnest, pleading eyes.

"We lost two but can save one. The best bet is to rub the orphan foal with..." Avery gestured to the pile of towels. "It transfers the scent. I'll waive the fee for tonight's services."

"You'll bring the colt here. Rub him down and offer him to Peach?"

Avery nodded.

"I bet that would make her feel better." Tory looked past him to Peach. "It'd make me feel better too. Go get him."

Tory muscled the stable door open. Snow drifted like dandelion seeds on a wish. The anticipation of new life had been exciting, the loss of the foals unbearably sad. But when Avery's colt had begun to nurse, the heaviness lifted. The wish was granted.

She tipped her face to the sky, opened her arms, and spun in slow, lazy circles. The dogs joined her and yipped out happy barks before engaging in a rambunctious chase. Delight bubbled inside of Tory like a child discovering a secret prize.

Avery leaned a hip against the barn door and studied Tory Keen, barely conscious, a hint of a smile on her face, twirling in the falling snow. Wee crystals dusted her hair and skin. He waited until the spinning dogs and woman slowed and came to a stop.

Tory wavered, a little fatigue drunk. She propped hands to her knees. "Whew, I'm dizzy. Remi, are you dizzy? How about you, Poncho?" They bathed her face in answer.

"What kind of name is Poncho for a dog?" Avery asked.

Tory scrubbed her hands over the fluffy fur. "A unique one, I guess. You'll have to ask Riley when he gets home. Poncho belongs to him."

Avery crouched. The pup rushed and tackled. He avoided Poncho's energetic tongue and smiled at Tory. "We deserve a case of champagne."

"The night certainly calls for something."

"You did good work in a tough situation."

"Right back at you, Doc."

"Would you mind if I bunked in the barn tonight? Peach should be monitored closely for the next three days."

"Occupational hazard spending nights in barns?"

Avery laughed, "Something like that."

"I expect you have a fresh change of clothes?" He nodded. "There is a shower in the loft, over the tack room. Help yourself." Tory pushed to her feet. "I'll sit with the new family until you're finished, and in the morning," she checked the time on her phone, "make that a few hours, Ginny will set out a first-rate breakfast."

"Not necessary."

"Don't let Ginny hear you," she laughed quietly. "Feeding us is a duty she takes very seriously."

Avery leaned heavily against the tiled wall and allowed the scorching spray to pound the strain from his bones. Adrenaline had fueled the past few hours. Its absence left him sluggish and numb.

If anyone would have told him he'd manage birth, death, and rebirth between midnight and dawn he'd have called them crazy.

He scrubbed away the exertion and emotion, pulled on soft jeans, and his favorite hoodie. His mood had greatly improved as he descended from the loft and strolled to the stall of miracles.

Avery found Tory slumped against the stable wall. A few feet away Peach and the colt rested contentedly. He stepped into the stall, opened his sleeping bag, and eased down next to Tory. She stirred as the straw shifted beneath her. Avery draped the heavy blanket across their legs. Tory twisted and pinned herself tight to his chest.

Her movement, innocent in motive, sparked a response which was solely male. Avery held still while she nestled in then levered her slightly upright to help her rest more comfortably.

Tory Keen, he thought as he looked down, was as beautiful as she was capable.

CHAPTER TWELVE

The sun flirted with the horizon as Dale strolled into the barn. The horses whinnied knowing breakfast would soon be served. The prior evening's sadness clung at the base of his skull like an obstinate headache. He reached into his pocket and palmed the sugar cubes he'd brought for Peach. A horse couldn't drown her sorrow in a gallon of Rocky Road after all.

Peach lifted her nose toward the candy man. Dale leaned over the half door, offered the treat then jolted. Resting in the straw at Peach's hooves, the same mare whose foals he had buried in the cold earth only hours before, was a jet-black colt. "Well I'll be a son of a monkey."

The next shock Dale discovered was Avery propped in the corner of the stall with Tory cozy beneath the crook of his arm. Rings of exhaustion darkened the soft tissue beneath closed eyes.

The boost of unexplained good fortune and morsel of buzz worthy tittle-tattle elevated Dale's mood. A cheerful melody chased away the cloud of grief. He whistled his way through the barn and decided to linger over the task of morning feeding.

A string of lyrics tickled the edge of Tory's consciousness. A tune just out of reach.

The tiny black colt surged to his feet. The commotion woke Tory. Her eyes fluttered open and she found herself nose to nose with the curious youngster. "Well hi there, how was your first night in my barn?"

"Pretty comfortable, all things considered." Avery said.

Tory had been so preoccupied with the foal she hadn't seen Avery. She masked her unease with a full wattage smile, and untangled her legs from the sleeping bag. She glanced warily at Avery. "Peach doing well?"

"She is." The colt bumped his hip, "and Titan seems right at home."

"Titan, huh?" Dale leaned over the door. "Never seen successful triplets before and he doesn't look like a newborn." Dale's eyes twinkled when they landed on Tory. "Guess the two of you had an interesting night."

Tory's face bloomed with color. She gathered the bulky blankets, and made her exit.

"Ginny always said the day you missed breakfast was the day you'd been up to no good," Dale heckled under his breath.

Tory quickened her pace. The men's conversation faded in her wake.

A tidy layer of snow greeted her along with the brisk punch of mountain air. Instantly clear-headed she covered the ground, stomped the snow from her boots, and thrust herself into the sanctity of home.

The fragrant kitchen welcomed her along with the strains of *Phantom of the Opera*. The keening melody pierced Tory's heart. She walked to Ginny and wrapped her arms around her waist.

"Good morning, Tory love," Ginny's lips twitched. "You have a bit of straw in your hair. Out carousing?"

Ginny fixed Tory a cup of lemon balm tea and listened to the details of the past six hours. "Call Ben Affleck – horror, heartbreak, and a happy ending, this has Oscar written all over it."

"Credits aren't rolling yet." Tory nipped a piece of Canadian bacon off the griddle. "Peach could still change her mind, reject Titan, or become ill. The delivery was brutal."

"You need a shower and a meal." Ginny shushed her out of the kitchen. "I'll send for Dale and Avery. Breakfast in twenty minutes."

"Imagine that, I'm not late after all."

Gathered at the farm table, conversations were replaced with clattering of silverware, audible gulps, and an occasional belch – the sweetest music to Ginny's ears. She leaned toward the window. "I love a springtime snow."

"Savor the flakes all fluffy and fresh, before they get trampled, melted and muddy." Dale leaned back in his chair and rubbed his belly like an expectant mother. "Hate to run, folks, but just because our day barely ended doesn't mean the next will pause and wait for us to catch up." He shoved to his feet and grinned at Avery. "If I push hard now I can squeeze in a quality nap later. Just don't tell the boss lady."

"Always stirring the pot," Ginny lifted Dale's plate and headed to the sink. Dale teased Ginny in his manner of gratitude for the breakfast. She dished the fun in equal turn until she had the final word and ushered him from her kitchen and into the snow.

Ginny returned to the table with another carafe of coffee.

The strenuous night hadn't left much color in Tory's cheeks. Ginny smirked, she'd fix that. "So Avery, you single?"

Tory's eyes shot like a laser to Ginny.

"I am."

"And your family? Where are they?"

Avery smiled at Ginny, "My mother lives in a small town, just outside of Philadelphia. She's an emergency room nurse but she also operates a bed-and-breakfast in the suburbs."

"Busy lady," Ginny nodded, "balancing a demanding career and operating a business."

"Equally fulfilling she assures me. I'll tell you this, you would make a few days easier if you'd share your recipe for the fare you whipped up here this morning."

Ginny blushed at the compliment. "Will you be traveling home for the summer?"

"Did you see how she dodged?" Tory laughed, "Ginny never shares her secrets."

"How do you expect me to maintain my allure in the kitchen if my secrets are tossed around to everyone who admires my cooking?" Ginny angled toward Avery and batted her lashes. "I need to dangle the bait to keep the fine looking gentleman coming to my table."

"Shameless," Tory's roll of eye didn't deter Ginny.

"Hush now girl, and pay attention. I'm discreetly digging for personal information. My skills extend beyond the stovetop."

Avery chuckled, "May I help clean up?"

"No, we've got it," Tory said.

"I've got it." Ginny corrected as she snatched Avery's plate and glass.

"My mom encouraged me to participate in setting the kitchen right after a meal. She says it helps to appreciate the hard work done by the cook."

"Difficult to argue with sound logic," Ginny set the dishes down and gestured for Avery to carry them into the kitchen. Together the trio worked to clear the table.

Ginny sat on a stool nursing a hot cup of coffee Avery had poured for her. She appreciated the ease with which Avery worked with Tory rinsing dishes and loading the dishwasher. "Where was I," her brow wrinkled in thought. "Oh yes, how is it you have come to Montana, Avery?"

"Internship program," Avery dropped silverware into the bin. "Part of the graduate curriculum includes an educational expansion rotation where students spend time with licensed vets all over the country." Avery flipped the dish towel over his shoulder. "I met Doc Webb at a veterinary conference. We hit it off." He laughed quietly. "The open bar helped. He agreed to the terms of the internship. Montana is my final rotation. I've been recruited to join a specialty orthopedic practice in Maryland. My position begins in two weeks."

"Why did you choose that specialty?"

"My Mom's dog tore ligaments in his rear leg. Not so long ago euthanasia would have been the only humane choice. Today there are countless treatment options making several life ending ailments a thing of the past. Look at what Doc Webb was able to do with those goats. Orthopedic and physical therapy applies to the animal kingdom too. What you do Tory," he wiggled his fingers in the air. "It has a vital place. I know holistic applications are supported behind closed doors. I think it's only a matter of time until the benefits are celebrated out loud."

"I don't need to be celebrated."

"Surly and a bit petulant following her night in the straw," Ginny peered over the frame of her glasses. She took the rag from Tory. "That's all the help I can handle. I've got floors to polish and you have work of your own. My breakfast gave you fuel but you both need some solid downtime." Ginny herded the pair toward the mudroom.

Avery lifted his coat from the peg and pulled it on.

Tory stepped into her boots, "Ginny can be a tad bossy." She straightened and blew a stray tendril from her eyes before tugging her hat in place.

Avery reached out and cupped her cheek. "I was impressed and appreciated your work with Peach." His thumb brushed the side of her face and idly traced the line of her jaw. His gentle touch, a direct contrast to his puckered brow. "But Ginny's right, you're beat." His hand fell away and gripped the door handle. "Try to get some shuteye," he muttered and strode into the morning.

Tory huffed and closed the door behind him. She knew she was tired. She knew it showed, but she didn't need a man to point it out. Especially a gorgeous, rumpled, smoldering, blue-eyed vet.

She thrust her arms into sleeves and drew the zipper to her neck. "Seventy-Six Trombones" and the cheer of *The Music Man* filled the air. Tory poked her head into the kitchen. Ginny stood at the just cleaned counter with potatoes, carrots, and onions lined up to face the cutting board. Next to the vegetables sat a slab of beef rubbed with dry seasoning.

"Ginny, what on earth?"

"Your dinner." She chunked the carrots at a pace which made Tory wince. "I realize the first act of digestion has just begun, but you will work in the stable straight through lunch." Ginny waved the knife at Tory daring her to contradict. "When you finally find your way into the house, imagine how it will smell."

"I'll spend the better part of my day dreaming about how it will taste."

Ginny chuckled.

Tory circled her head in an attempt to relieve the weariness clenching her shoulders like talons.

"Can you take a minute and lay down? Just for a half hour."

"After Cora's lesson I will."

Ginny's lips pursed.

"I promise," Tory hurried to assure her. "I'll have a cup of tea and sit for twenty whole minutes."

"You need more than twenty and sitting is not prone."

"The tea and a hearty serving of your stew will be the best remedy."

CHAPTER THIRTEEN

"Miss Tory, Miss Tory," Cora rushed into the barn. Blonde pigtails poked from beneath her orange riding cap. Her breeches were turquoise and her chamois shirt dotted with hot pink balloons. "It's my big day."

"Big day, huh? What day is that?"

Her lip jutted out. "It's my birthday. I am ten."

"Of course I remember. You are practically a grown up." Tory tugged Cora's earlobe and counted to ten.

Cora giggled. "You can come to my party. Mom got chocolate peanut butter cake and grape popsicles." She spun in a circle. "My very best favorites."

"Sounds delicious, we'll see."

"I heard you saved a orphan last night. That's the greatest. I get it if you have to stay with him tonight."

Tory patted her capped head. "Get Star out and groom him. I moved him to the front of the barn."

"Aren't the front stalls for the private owners?"

"Yes, someone's interested in him. They're driving in at the end of the week to look him over."

Cora's shoulders slumped so quickly Tory thought she'd topple over. Her boots scuffed the floor as she walked the length of the stable. Instantly the girl perked and skipped the remaining twenty feet to join Avery at the end of the barn. Tory watched Cora bounce and chatter in excited syllables about her birthday.

Avery walked toward Tory. "That's a whole lot of color decorating a very small human being. Nice to see her enthusiasm at such a young age."

"Cora's special," Tory smiled. "She's going to remember this day for her entire life."

"Turning ten's a big deal for girls?"

"Double digits? Of course," Tory peeked over her shoulder to be sure Cora was out of hearing range. "But not as big as owning your first horse." Her whisper barely contained her anticipation. "Cora's parents bought Star. They are planning to surprise her after her lesson."

Avery whistled low, "Nice gift."

"I wouldn't have agreed if Cora and Star weren't an absolute match. She will smile for years." Tory walked past Avery into the barn office. "I'm placing an order for supplies. Anything I should add for Peach or Titan?"

"Nothing special," Avery slanted his hip against the door frame. "Peach isn't showing any post labor complications. Examination of the placenta confirmed no abnormalities."

"Good." Tory booted up the computer.

"I had a brief internet conference with Doc Webb. Aside from being sickened at the twin bombshell, he agreed that Peach's premature labor was her body's method of protecting her."

Tory frowned, "Shouldn't have bothered him on his trip, but of course he'd want to be in the loop." Vacant eyes scanned emails. "I want to get a few things done before Cora's lesson." Tory immediately regretted her dismissing tone but she shouldn't have to apologize for being a competent business owner.

She was irritated and trying to run him off again. He studied her profile. There was no residual sign of the arduous evening they had shared. Avery pushed closer, hitched his hip on the corner of her desk. He smothered his grin when she huffed. He studied her stern expression. "I'm feeling confident the fostering will be successful."

"The next two days will tell the story." Tory knew she was being rude. But she wanted his compassionate tone, not to mention his long denim clad legs out of her office. "If you need anything to make the loft more comfortable, ask Dale. He'll take care of it."

"Ok," Avery shifted his knee when Tory reached to open a desk drawer. "Statistics dictate a traumatic labor will disrupt the maternal bonding of mare and foal." He continued on unhurried. "The simple fact Peach was willing to allow Titan to nurse without rebuffing him is a stroke in our favor."

Fatigue softened Tory's defenses. "Rejection would be more devastating than burying the stillborns." She tucked her chin and avoided Avery's gaze while her eyes filled.

Avery checked his desire to comfort her. He straightened and leaned back. "Have a good lesson."

Cora carried her saddle and bridle to the tack room. While she was occupied, Tory walked Star out of the stable and helped Cora's mother secure a pink dotted bow around his neck. Tory grabbed her camera and hitched her arms over the rail of the paddock. The little girl's squeals of joy raced across the acres until the mountains returned the joyful sound.

Finally Cora's parents lured her away to attend her party at a local restaurant.

Snow was falling again. Tory glanced at the sky full with clouds burdened with moisture. The weatherman's prediction of late afternoon squalls ending with a shake of Mother Nature's fist may come true.

She grabbed a broom and cleared the concrete in front of the barn. She wouldn't gamble with a chance of someone slipping. The dogs chased the powder like children, then jumped up, and began barking excitedly. "Who in the devil? Hush... hush now." Tory looked toward the lane and spotted Maggie's car.

Tory allowed Remi and Poncho to deliver their welcome.

"Good evening, canines." Maggie hopped from the cab and indulged them with a hearty rub.

Tory pulled the zipper on her jacket a little higher. "What are you up to?"

"It snows, I bake." Maggie lifted two pies from the rear compartment.

"It's a spring squall, Maggie, and you don't have to make up excuses. You bake all the time."

Maggie lifted a shoulder. "The grapevine has reported last night's vile delivery." Maggie looked at her friend. "You are on your last dredge of energy."

"I am," Tory didn't bother to hide her exhaustion. "I promised Ginny I'd eat and endure a twenty minute nap after Cora left."

"Then in we go. I'll not interfere with Ginny's orders." Maggie stomped off her boots, strolled comfortably into the kitchen, and set the pies on the counter.

Tory snapped open the corner of the container and groaned in anguish. "You are a mean, mean friend."

Maggie laughed. "You won't go hungry. Anyway it gives you an excuse to burrow in and make vats of tea or cocoa and enjoy your quiet house." Maggie pointed out the window. "Look at your cottage all dusted with snow, beautiful. The weather guessers are predicting another few inches overnight."

Tory smiled and dipped the ladle into the cast-iron pot. "You want a bowl?"

"No thanks, but can I have a tour? I know you're supposed to rest."

"I've passed the point of needing a nap and needing a solid night's sleep." Tory sat her stew on the island. "It's too hot. We'll let it cool. Don't tell Ginny."

Maggie drew her finger in an X across her heart.

"It hasn't changed too much. I've only had time to add a few bits of furniture."

"Stop teasing." Maggie grabbed Tory's hand and tugged toward the breezeway. "Ooooo," she moaned not too unlike the anguish Tory expressed over the fresh baked pie. "It's just like a little snow globe, isn't it?"

"Funny, I was thinking the same earlier." Tory opened the door leading into the heart of the home.

"You are rushing me." Maggie sat in the rocker and gave a gentle push with her toes. "Hmmm... give me the latest Nora Roberts, a glass of wine, and don't come bothering me."

Tory laughed.

"You will need a sign that says just that to hang on the door." Maggie stood and turned a full circle absorbing every drop of the completed room. There was a cozy oversized chair with an afghan folded neatly on the arm. She rubbed the material between her thumb and index finger, "This one of your Nana's?"

"I stole it like a thief out of the linen closet."

"Not stealing if it belongs to you," Maggie gave Tory's arm a light pinch and strolled along a built-in bookcase. Wide planks of raw aged wood stretched across the wall.

Magazines, Tory's drug of choice, were arranged in file boxes. Novels, fiction and non, hardcover and trade paperbacks sat in boxes on the floor waiting to be shelved. Another tote held black and white vintage images of the ranch and her grandparents. There were more with Murphy and Tory as children, and still dozens of color prints, bold and full of the vibrant lives of the rescues. A framed lineage, of grandchildren, nieces and nephews, equine, canine, and human. "Your family." Maggie grinned and lifted a candid shot of Tory with Smooch. His furry llama lips pressed firmly against hers. "Everyone has a weird uncle." She laughed fully.

Tory led Maggie into the kitchen. "Seems even smaller with the appliances in."

Maggie rubbed her palms gleefully, mischief brightened her eyes. "I must root in your cabinets and invade your privacy as only a best friend can." She reached up and with a grand flourish opened the cherry doors. She clucked her tongue. "Momma Hubbard? Your cupboards are bare. We need to fill your pantry."

"I figured I'd just raid Ginny's stash."

"Dangerous messing about in someone's surplus, we'll go into town."

"Ugh, shopping," Tory whined.

"Better idea," Maggie snapped her finger. "I'll stock you up and call it housewarming."

"Not necessary."

"It most certainly is, unless you want a houseplant to torture and kill. Or worse I could give you a hideous decorative lamp or knickknack you'll feel obligated to display so you don't hurt my feelings."

"In that case, food works for me."

"Your cottage is perfect. It just feels like it's always been your home. Don't you think?"

"I do," Tory agreed.

"When you breaking it in?"

"Who knows?' her palms lifted and fell. Her schedule for the next several days would wreak havoc on her resolute timeline. "I have to move the larger furniture in from the main house, then my clothes."

Maggie squatted down beside the counter to nose through the bedroom ensemble Tory had selected. "These are so soft and dreamy. Aren't you going to love sinking into inches of cumulous clouds after a day in the barn?"

It was exactly what Tory had pictured when she'd chosen the delicate eyelet coverlet in white of all colors. Far from sensible for a ranch girl like her. She'd chalked the extravagance up to her weakened state following her retail excursion. Another few days sitting in the bags with sales tags attached, and Tory would return the lot. She would rummage through the sale rack and opt for no-nonsense cotton sheets. And since most days her body was caked in earth or worse she'd find a comforter the shade of soil.

"It's beautiful," Tory ran her hand over the bedspread, "too beautiful for... NO!"

Maggie snapped the price tag off the delicate material. "You are not returning it."

Tory's horrified gasp was muddled with a sparkle of laughter. "You are insane."

"Actually Pot, be grateful your best friend Kettle," she pointed her thumb to her chest, "can hear the maracas knocking around in your head. Tell me truthfully," her eyes narrowed. "Were you not this very second, allowing practical Tory to talk you into exchanging the feminine and indulgent for the non-fanciful and plain?" Maggie tugged out the sheets next. "Ooo, 1000 count…heaven," the tag disconnected with a crack.

Tory grimaced as Maggie jammed the price ticket into her pocket. "Pass me the dust ruffle." Tory wiggled her fingers at her friend.

Maggie lifted a skeptical brow then handed the package to Tory.

She chewed her lip for an instant then ripped the price off the frivolous cloth.

Maggie hooted, "That's my girl."

The friends walked back to the glass room. Snow was falling faster. "I adore you but," Maggie hooked her arm through Tory's, "I'm out of here. I have batter to mix, icing to whip."

Remi and Poncho started to bark again. "Now who's here?"

Maggie peeked about the window, "Big rig, dark blue, never seen it before." She pushed her nose against the pane, let out a low whistle. "As you love to say, another day, another carpenter. Yum Yum."

Tory bumped her hip against Maggie. "Turns out he isn't a carpenter. Avery is the vet covering for Doc Webb." She heaved a sigh and walked to the counter mumbling. "Sexy, rumpled, bossy, veterinary intern Avery. Why can't you ever make things I don't like to eat?" Tory turned with a scowl.

A knowing smirk painted Maggie's face, "Dish."

"Dish what?"

"Intern Avery, that's what."

"He's learning the ropes of a Midwestern vet, then moving on to his permanent job in Maryland."

"And?"

"And nothing," Tory shrugged. "He's filling in for Doc Webb while he's on his anniversary trip. He managed Peach's delivery last night which I'll tell you about another time. Happy ending hasn't washed away the chill yet." Tory trembled. "He's good. Better than Doc Webb's rave review. Avery is beyond competent, patient under duress, and he loves and admires his mother."

Maggie folded her arms over her chest. Her toes tapped with staccato impatience. "Those are the facts plus a bit of intriguing personal, but I want the sexy, rumpled, bossy part that goes along with the story."

Tory waved a hand dismissing her, "We just rub each other."

"Yea baby, that's what I'm after." Maggie eased her hip onto the stool by the bar. "The yummy part, my oven can hold a few more minutes."

Tory noted the mischief in Maggie's eyes. "No yum. Get out, bake cake, whip icing."

Maggie sashayed toward the mudroom. "I get it," she slid her arms into her coat. "I can take a hint and I certainly don't stay where I'm not wanted."

"Now just hold it," Tory followed Maggie into the snow.

Maggie pulled open the truck door and tossed Tory a playful wink. "You and Mr. Sexy Rumpled have a good visit."

"He's not visiting, he's..." Tory stood shivering on the stoop. "Some friend," she commented to the dogs. Remi cocked her head to the side, tongue lolling out of her mouth.

Poncho levered toward the snow in an impressive downward dog and slid sideways into the fluffy snow. He completed his snow yoga with a frolic wiggle on his back.

Tory herded the dogs inside and settled at the counter with her stew. Her body was rebelling against the day's trials with a surge of adrenaline. "How do you guys feel about watching me heft some furniture?" Remi's head stayed on the floor while Poncho chased his tail in infinite circles.

Tory tidied the kitchen then dropped her iPod into the dock. She cued up eighty's hair-bands, jacked the volume to inappropriate and *Knockin' on Heaven's Door* filled the room.

CHAPTER FOURTEEN

Avery's boots scarcely cleared the earth beneath them. Weary beyond explanation, he was desperate for a hot shower, clean clothes, and sleep. Intent on retrieving his duffle and climbing the steps to the loft over Keen stables he walked out of the barn.

The grounds of the ranch were silent and dark. Horses and humans tucked in for the night. He looked toward the house where the lady of the manor slept. Capable, independent, and slightly susceptible, Tory Keen. Her autonomy should be a turn off but the glimpse at vulnerability this afternoon had him itching to expose another guarded layer.

A light burned in the breezeway off the main house. A figure moved into view.

"Unbelievable," Avery shook his head and watched Tory wiggle her hips before muscling the massive table another few feet.

He changed direction, and crossed toward the cottage. "Does the woman ever take a break?" The strains of *Every Rose has its Thorn* vibrated the glass room. Avery raised his fist and wrapped his knuckles hard against the panes.

Tory jumped, pressed her hand to her chest. She laughed, visibly relaxed and pointed to the cottage door. "It's open."

Once inside the small structure Avery toed off his boots and raised his voice over the music. "You have to be worn-out. I feel like I'm auditioning for the Walking Dead."

Tory located her device and lowered the music. "I've been cast in the leading role."

"You should be in bed, not moving hunks of wood by yourself."

"I'm more than capable." She thrust her chin, "And this is not a piece of timber. This is my Nana's canning table." For Tory, each knife gouge and kettle burn symbolized love of hearth and home.

"Not arguing capability," Avery held up his palms in defense. "I'm offering to help." He ran a light touch over the scarred butcher-block top. "Will you allow me to move a few things for you?"

Tory studied him and saw the offer for what it was. A genuine gift of manpower. "With me."

Avery lifted an end and walked backwards into the cottage.

"Left. My left," Tory giggled.

"Here?"

"Yes."

Avery inspected the renovation. Top notch carpentry, and a meticulous plan created a seamless marriage of old and new. The design amplified the beauty of the small structure. His hand trailed along the mantle. He bent down and admired the pot belly stove.

"Wood or pellet?"

"Wood."

He nodded and strolled to the kitchen. Scattered across the bar, images of items cut out of magazines and printed from the internet were carefully pasted together in collage layouts for each room. "Visual and organized."

"Say what you mean," Tory walked to the refrigerator and removed a pitcher of water. "I'm anal."

Avery snorted, "I was thinking a planner. Know what you want and only take the next step forward, when you're sure."

Tory didn't care for his accurate pegging of her personality. "I like magazines. I love the tidy pictures, the pristine rooms."

"Wasn't a crack." Avery studied her. "What else are you planning to reposition tonight?"

"Just a few things, it's no trouble."

Avery noticed the stack of blankets and pillows at the foot of the steps. He recognized the name of the linen, bed, and bath store on the shopping bags. "Are you sleeping in here tonight?"

Tory looked at the stacked comfort, felt it beckon. "I have a vision in my mind for christening the springhouse."

"I don't see it here," he shuffled the paper mockups. "Tell me."

Her eyes narrowed at his ribbing. "I want a long bath followed by quiet time in my rocking chair in my snow globe walk through."

"That doesn't sound…"

She held her finger up silencing him. "I want a quilt on my lap, and a dog at my feet. I want to sip a fresh squeezed, sea salt rimmed, top shelf margarita, while I savor the final pages of my novel." A satisfied cat-captured-the-canary smile softened her features.

"Wow, that is a list."

"I have everything except the tequila." She strolled to the bookcase and lifted a thick hardcover novel. "I've been saving the final forty pages for my first night. Do you have any idea how hard it is to not finish the last pages of your favorite novelist's most recent installment in her award winning series?"

"I don't read."

Tory mocked a knife to her heart. "Anyway, a face down flop on top of my carefully selected comforter was not what I pictured." She sighed, "Idyllic expectations beg for disappointment."

"Does it have to be perfect?"

She lifted her shoulder.

"Tory," he said quietly. "It's been a long day for both of us. We're both tired. The brand of tired that fuels a fierce second wind then leaves you flat-out drained. I will help you put things in the vicinity of where you want them. Then I'll disappear to the barn like a good minion."

"The rescue," Tory's eyes popped wide. "That was you?"

He shrugged. "So as you know from firsthand experience, I can follow instructions and get out of your hair and be helpful somewhere else." Avery grinned at her embarrassment. "Let's get to it, boss."

CHAPTER FIFTEEN

They shoved, hauled, pushed and tugged and relocated nearly everything Tory had hoped to transfer from the main house. Avery backed into the room and placed the small three-drawer dresser along the wall. He turned and faced the dark wooden head and footboard of her bed, the frame assembled, minus the box spring and mattress.

"Comfortable."

"I know my limits. The mattress and box spring are at the top of the steps in the main house. I will not risk death or damage for a soft sleep tonight. At this point any flat surface will do."

"I don't believe you." Avery tipped his head to the side. "What's two more pieces at this point?"

Resigned she led him to the foyer and the beautiful staircase. "If we lose our grip…"

"We won't."

They took it easy and within a few minutes settled the box spring into place. Tory lifted her thumb to her lips and nibbled nervously.

"You bought one of those ruffle things didn't you?"

She nodded.

"Put it on. Makes more sense than taking the bed apart again tomorrow."

He strode from the room. Tory hustled to spread the accent piece into place. Satisfied she turned and found Avery at the opening to her bedroom with the mattress propped at his hip.

"Swallow your protest, Keen, it's done. Grab an end and let's finish."

Delight sparkled in Tory's eyes as the mattress fell with a thud. Face highlighted with raw pleasure she lifted her knee to crawl atop the naked mattress.

Avery's mouth quirked.

Tory hopped back. "You've more than earned a beer."

"No argument." Avery followed her to the kitchen. "It's a nice space."

"It will be, yes." Tory clicked her bottle to his. "Thank you." The cold liquid flooded her throat. "Now, if I can shower without drowning."

The idea of her collapsing in the steam overrode Avery's thoughts of her undressed and dripping wet. "How about I lifeguard?" He chuckled when her mouth dropped open. "From the kitchen," he clarified. "Seriously, get cleaned up while I finish my beer. I'll rest easier knowing you haven't passed out and whacked your head."

"Really that's not..."

"Tory, I'm going to enjoy my beer," he gestured with his bottle. "I'll listen until the water shuts off, then head to the barn."

She pressed her lips together. The line of her jaw drew taut as she considered.

"Go, without a fight please." His soft tone had more effect than a demand.

She hurried from the room without another word.

Avery rolled his neck and shoulders, looked over the room. He could see her here. In the vision so sleekly arranged. Meticulous diagrams mapping colors and textures, furniture and art... the personal touches to a home that would be innately Tory.

The shower surged to life, the exhaust fan hummed. Avery tipped the bottle and drained his beer. He shifted on tired legs toward the sink. His foot knocked the bag of linens and the pillow skidded across the floor. He lifted the plush cushion.

Every tidy detail, he smiled.

Completely Tory.

Tory would indulge another time. Avery was as tired as she. He needed to get to the barn and rest. "The barn," she groaned. Lavender shampoo slid between her shoulder blades. She could at least offer him the spare room in the main house. He wasn't her guest. Not even her friend really. For goodness sake he was barely an acquaintance. Still it would be the hospitable thing to do. She turbaned her hair in a fluffy yellow towel and pulled on her oversized t-shirt and yoga pants. She decided she was decent enough to converse with a man who's barely an acquaintance. She slipped her feet into moccasins and opened the door.

"I'm alive." She walked toward the kitchen. "Avery?" His empty bottle was in the sink. She glanced out the window. The light was burning in the bunk room over the barn. Already gone. Better than a pajama clad goodbye.

Tory closed the breezeway door. She strolled through the cottage, flicked lights out as she went. The dogs lounged, settled and snoring. Tory lifted the blanket from the love seat. She'd deal with making the bed tomorrow. Tonight she'd wrap herself up and sleep like the dead until... she gaped in awestruck silence as she entered her room.

Her bed... straight out of the picture. The eyelet comforter tucked neatly beneath the trio of color punch pillows. Tory trailed her hand over the perfect comforter. If her heart wasn't pounding so hard against her ribs she would have sworn she was dreaming.

Propped on the dresser, the image she'd trimmed from the magazine with a note beside it.

Sleep well,
Avery

CHAPTER SIXTEEN

Tory ran her fingers along the twin bed frame in the loft over the barn. The blankets were folded and stacked in an orderly pile. Avery's three-night vigil over Peach and Titan had come and gone. Mom and foal were happy and healthy. She scooped up the bedding and walked to the cedar chest. Her boots echoed in the hollow room. Tory lifted the lid and set the blankets inside.

She hadn't seen Avery for two days. He was busy covering the clinic and making calls all over the county. There hadn't been any problems with her rescues, or the pregnant mares. Tory rapped her knuckles on the sturdy wood. "No need to be tempting the gods of chaos."

She descended the steps to the barn below. Dale pushed the feeding bin toward the next group of stalls. "When's your flight to Denver?"

"Driving directly to the airport from the hearing."

"Cutting it close, don't you think?"

Tory shrugged. "Get in, get out."

The conference stretched all week linking educational presentations with expensive dinners and fancy speakers.

Tory knew she should go early and stay longer, rubbing elbows with industry leaders, but it wasn't in her nature.

But first things first, the hearing.

The overnight dusting of snow dissolved under the persistent rays of the morning sun. The damp road matched Tory's mood. She drove toward the magistrate's office. With Doc Webb out of town Tory would present the preliminary report to the court. The judge would make a decision and the legal course would begin.

She parked her truck away from the other vehicles. Her heartbeat shifted from a bass drum's steady thud to a snare's fanatical tap. She hated this part. Legal jargon and lawyers posturing and jockeying. The process worked most of the time but Tory preferred to stick to the tangible. Caring for and fostering the animals.

She closed her eyes, quieted her mind, and steadied her pulse. She'd take a moment to skim the thick file on the seat beside her. Tory knew the information cold, but understood the consequences of a single contradicted fact.

Poised and ready, she walked to the building.

Avery selected a chair at the back of the magistrate's office. His presence was not required but Webb had suggested, if his schedule allowed, he sit in and see how the entire system played out.

Tory was on the stand. The woman Avery had observed during their random encounters was masked beneath appropriate courtroom attire. Her hair tied back, in a manner he assumed Tory would consider practical, only amped her beauty.

Her passion and anger held taut as the reins of a saddled stallion. She laid out the events of the rescue in succinct steps while the man responsible vibrated with fury a few feet away. Tory never acknowledged him. She simply answered question after question, then submitted video records and veterinary findings into the official record.

Tory was excused. She stepped down and exited the courtroom. Avery watched the defendant snarl as she passed in unwavering strides. His attorney offered a placating pat to his wrist.

Tory's eyes flicked to Avery as she opened the door to exit. Her head dipped in slight acknowledgement. He rose and followed her into the lobby. She continued her rapid exit. "Need air."

Avery kept pace and noted the sheen bathing her face. He gripped her elbow and was surprised when she didn't resist.

"Other side of the truck." Her words puffed. She put the steel between her body and the office building.

Once she'd achieved the slightest speck of privacy she trembled and broke. She folded at the waist, braced hands to knees as her breath rushed in a torrent.

The composure on the stand had cost her. Avery's hand went to her back and rubbed. He prayed her release would not contain tears.

Tory garbled a mantra to gather herself. From her bent position she offered Avery a weak smile. "Thanks for that."

"You're welcome?"

She laughed and stood. "As much as I'd like to explain my split personality I have a flight to catch." She tugged open her door and climbed behind the wheel. Tory touched two fingers to her temple and saluted Avery.

Avery jammed his hands into his pockets as Tory gunned the engine and headed out of the lot. He'd collected another piece in the intricate puzzle that was Tory Keen.

CHAPTER SEVENTEEN

Tory scanned the faces assembled in the room. It was her third year presenting the advantages of using holistic and massage therapy techniques to heal animals, post trauma. Every year attendance at her segments grew as the interest in her practice gained popularity.

Tory had requested a weekday with consecutive timeslots. She often felt she was just getting warmed up by the end of the first session. From experience, she'd learned attendees who were serious stayed in their seats and benefited by the expanded discussion during the second hour.

The other bonus of presenting on Thursday was cheap flights and no added expense for overnight accommodations.

"Get in, get out." Tory muttered and opened her laptop and cued the PowerPoint.

"Ms. Keen, a moment?" A man wearing a suit tailored for the Trump Tower boardroom joined her at the podium. "I represent Grey Stone Plantation. I have a business proposal I wish to present to you."

Tory opened her portfolio, selected a folder of notes. "I'm starting in five minutes."

"I only need two."

Tory uncapped her water bottle and measured the man. Egotistical, with purse strings to match, and inevitably accustomed to getting his way. "You may have two, after my lecture."

His indignant huff was smoothed easily with a flash of cosmetic dentistry. He reached into his lapel pocket and produced a business card. "Until then," he placed it on the lectern and selected a seat in the back of the room.

Tory's group was attentive and asked great questions. A few inquired about private workshops, internships and hands-on learning. The idea intrigued Tory. Certainly something to think about.

The room cleared and Mr. Power Suit man remained. He hadn't glanced up during her spiel. Not a single image or statistic had enticed his eyes to leave the screen in front of him.

Tory tidied the computer cables for the next presenter. She noticed the man had stowed his work as well.

"You have no further obligations with the conference this evening," he stated. "I've arranged for a table with the best view of the mountains. Allow me to lay out Grey Stone Plantation's proposal over dinner?"

"My duties in Denver are fulfilled, yes. But I'm returning to Montana this evening. I don't have time for dinner."

"I can arrange a flight first thing tomorrow. Will you hear me out? Grey Stone will cover your expenses in Denver and compensate you for the intrusion to your schedule." He met Tory's stunned silence with a confident tip of his head. He lowered his voice and added, "You do understand what the exposure and affiliation with Grey Stone Plantation would do for your trade?"

Tory did. She really did, and if she'd allow her annoyance to slide a fraction she'd admit she was starving. "The first flight out of Denver."

He fixated on his iPhone a brief moment then slipped the device into his pocket. "The confirmation should be in your email."

Tory's brows lifted. She opened her phone and sure enough she would be returning to Montana, first class no less, at 6:15 AM. Not sure if she should be impressed or frightened, Tory nodded and followed his polished loafers to the exclusive terrace restaurant.

Tory sat at the bar. Her head spinning more from Grey Stone's pitch than the liquor in her vodka tonic. Big money looking for a reputed equine massage therapist to work with their race horses throughout each leg of the Triple Crown.

She swirled her ice, punctured her lime with her cocktail straw. Three year old thoroughbreds, three races, three cities and... She raised the glass and drained the clear liquid.

And a one hundred thousand dollar paycheck.

CHAPTER EIGHTEEN

Avery's brain was a jumble of statistics and cited case files. He followed the mass of people exiting the auditorium. Not in the mood for polite conversation, he planned to snag a few bottles of beer, head upstairs, and order room service.

The crowd parted. Avery entered the dim bar and stopped cold.

Tucked on a corner stool, legs crossed at the knee, exposing miles of flesh ending with thin blue straps holding sculpted wood to arched feet... Tory Keen.

The shoes added inches of overkill to her incredible legs. Like a desert traveler spotting an oasis, Avery drooled. Solitude forgotten, he strode across the room and claimed the vacant stool beside her. "Of all the bars in all the land."

Tory's startled gasp ended with a snicker. "He walked into mine." She scanned his sport coat and tie. "Grown up clothes look good on you."

"Back at you." Avery signaled the bartender. His eyes trailed over her legs as he loosened his tie. He tipped his head toward her event ID on the bar. "I didn't know you were presenting. I would have sat in." He whimpered when the frosted glass of beer appeared in front of him. "I've earned a few of these, let me tell you."

"What session did you attend?"

"Ethics in business."

"Fun."

"The Maryland practice set up my trip. They foot the bill, they choose the sessions." He shrugged. "Tell me, what's driven you to drink? The stress of lecturing? Unruly, unappreciative attendees?"

"I was heading home when I got an invitation to dinner, a complimentary hotel room, and an opportunity of a lifetime."

Avery turned fully toward her. The proximity of the stool placed his knees on either side of hers. "Elucidate."

Tory chuckled, "Great word."

"I've just left an hour lecture on the importance of clarification."

Tory lifted her drink, eyed him over the rim, and attempted to settle the nerves that had taken up Zumba in her belly. "Big money racehorse owner wants me to rub his purse fatteners." Tory patted the envelope beside her. "Imagine me, the traveling massage therapist for Grey Stone Plantation during the three legs of the Triple Crown."

"Wow. You should be drinking champagne."

"Haven't said yes yet."

"You will."

"So you survived your first week as a Montana vet."

"Some week," Avery chuckled, "emergency births, orphaned foals, nurse mares, with a side of spay and neuter."

"I'd love to tell you the events of this week were out of the ordinary, but we handle what comes. And what comes is rarely scheduled."

"Cheers to that." Avery tapped his bottle to her glass.

The bartender freshened their drinks.

Tory stared at the cocktail. "My face is partially numb. I don't think I should have another."

"Stay a little longer?"

What was she going to do in her room? "Tell me more about your position in Maryland."

His eyes lit with fun, "Haven't said yes yet."

"But you will," Tory tossed his words back.

Avery talked about the specialty practice. His anticipation of participating in cutting edge medicine, his eagerness to expand his skills filled their cocoon of space in the crowded bar. The tension of the day slipped away. Before she knew it, ice rattled in the bottom of her cup.

"Now I've done it."

Avery laughed quietly.

"I know my limit and I'm over it, by two. You need to deliver me to my room, Avery. Right now."

He stood, offered a hand to help her from her stool.

Tory swayed but righted just as quickly. "Please put your arm around me so I don't topple in these damn shoes."

"Meant to compliment those when I sat down." Her flushed face tipped toward his. "Your shoes...hot." He scooped her purse and papers off the bar and pulled her tight against his side. "I won't have you making a scene."

Avery guided her to the elevator, occupied with chattering conference attendees on the way to evening sessions.

"Floor?"

"Eleven. Key's in my purse." Tory leaned her head on his shoulder and whispered. "Thanks for driving me home."

He opened the door to her room and walked her in. He released her at the foot of the bed and tossed her purse on the dresser. He turned and she was there...too close. Her stilts aligned her hips perfectly with his. Avery hissed and took a step in retreat.

Tory's hands shot out and hooked his belt loops. "One kiss," she murmured as the gap between them vanished. "We won't go to Hades for one little kiss."

"We might," he muttered then guided his lips to hers. The sweetness cost him. Tory sighed, went limp. Avery gathered her close, lifted her and laid her across the bed. Glazed eyes fluttered. He slipped off her shoes and pressed his thumbs against her arches. First one then the other.

Tory moaned softly, a siren's song.

Avery pulled the comforter over her and walked to the window. Beyond the glass, the city raced at a tempo akin to his heart. He leaned his forehead to the oversized pane and exhaled. He closed the blinds then turned and indulged in one last look. The sight tilted him more effectively than the alcohol swimming in his blood. Facing certain peril Avery moved to the edge of the bed. He brushed the strand of hair away from her face and traced his fingertips from her temple to chin. She stirred, snuggled deeper into the pillow. Minimizing the budding risks, for Tory as well as himself, Avery fled to certain safety.

His own room, two floors below.

CHAPTER NINETEEN

Tory appreciated the early flight to Denver. She was grateful for the indulgent privacy first class provided. She refused the mimosa and opted for plain orange juice, toast, and a dose of extra strength Tylenol.

She had flashes from the previous night. Avery had escorted her to her hotel room. She was fairly certain there had been a kiss, but the rest was fuzzy. She'd woken in her bed with a throbbing head and no shoes.

She intended to call him when she arrived home. But what would she say? Sorry I jumped you then passed out? Regardless, one hour had rolled to the next. The time for a casual phone call had expired. Avery had sessions at the conference until the afternoon. He'd be back in her zip code tonight.

Tory would have to gear up for a face-to-face.

Dale whistled "Amazing Grace" as he maneuvered the length of the barn scooping feed into the horses' buckets. There may have been a hymn on his lips but the muscles in his jaw were clenched. Tory leaned against the stable door and waited for him to exit the enclosure.

"Back from Denver already? Thought maybe they talked you into an extra session."

"No chance. I did get a five-star dinner and a big money offer to handle some race horses during the Triple Crown. More travel in my immediate future, I'm afraid. Sorry the timing can't be helped."

"We'll manage." Dale opened a stall door and removed a pail, added a scoop of grain. "You do know those races are held on the other side of the Mississippi River."

"Har, har, enough pleasantries, I can feel the bad news vibrating off you."

"Ariel's owner is petitioning to have his livestock returned." Dale jammed the bolt closed and secured the stall.

"Of course he is. Heaven forbid we trample his rights as a human being." Tory sighed. "What are you holding back?"

Dale scrubbed his hand across his face. "The seizure on Ariel may not hold."

"The hell it won't." Tory's fingers balled into tight fists. "Equine Advocates were all over this a few days ago. Pushing the rescue footage and Doc Webb's report."

"The guy hooked a shark attorney. He is making noise about the Keen Ranch writing the rules as they go. Getting what they want even if lying and stealing is the way of it."

Tory kicked a bale of straw and clamped down on her need to scream. "Nonsense and double talk."

"His legal rep claims the photos and video are fake, or at the very least embellished."

"Doc Webb amputated the goats' legs for effect. I tell you, Dale, as long as idiots can inhale, the world will have to deal with the rubbish they exhale."

Tory sat heavily. Her hands dove into her flame hair. She rolled her shoulders and absorbed the sounds and scents around her. The horses shifted their weight muffled by the cushion of bedding at their feet. Tory breathed deep, calming now, as her brain worked toward a positive, productive solution.

She jammed her hat on her head, called the dogs. "I'm going for a walk." The exercise would raise her endorphins. She hoped they'd work their reputed hormone magic and improve her mood.

The crisp morning air filled her lungs and puffed in short bursts like a steam engine. Remi and Poncho trotted beside her, each with a gnawed stick clenched between their teeth. Tory knew the solution to the problem facing the courts, but she wasn't ready to choke it down.

Light snow dusted the dew soaked grass like confectioners' sugar reminding Tory Maggie would be dropping off pastry for her brother's welcome home dinner. At least the premium baked goods would provide calorie comfort.

Remi and Poncho barked and bounded across the field.

Maggie knelt in the wet grass to rub and pat. "What a nice greeting," she chuckled then grinned at Tory. "Good morning, globe-trotter."

"A one day trip to Denver is hardly a world tour."

"I'd kill to go anywhere." Maggie took the stick from Remi and gave it a mighty toss. "You spent the night unexpectedly, Ginny tattled. She also said you showed up this morning hung-over." Maggie clucked her tongue, and then sent Poncho's stick flying. "A good friend should wait patiently for you to share your tale of juicy over-indulgence." Maggie slid her arm through Tory's. "But patience is a virtue God forgot to bless me with." Her laughter raced over the meadow as wild as the dogs. "I'm here to extract every last detail, and I'll warn you, I'm prepared to take extreme measures."

"Chocolate croissant extreme?"

"I'm wicked."

Tory and Maggie walked into the house. At the stove Ginny hummed a ballad from *Cats*. Her glasses clung to the tip of her nose while she sprinkled fresh herbs into a simmering pot. "You found her."

"Right where you told me," Maggie tittered. "I often wonder how you know everything."

"Magic powers," Tory sat heavily in the ladder back chair. "Will you let me borrow a smidge of your superpowers, Ginny?"

"Dale told me about the appeal." Ginny washed her hands. "You know how to clear that particular hurdle without any fancy tricks." She slipped the apron off and hooked it on the peg beside the stove. "I'm off to ladies' luncheon. We're playing Bingo, and I'm feeling lucky."

Tory rose and wrapped her arms around Ginny. "I've left you alone to prepare for Murphy's welcome home dinner. I'm sorry."

"Your plate has been full. Don't fret, tomorrow morning you'll do your share." She winked, "I have a list."

Tory paled.

Ginny wound a scarf around her neck and pulled on her coat. "I set a timer for the soup. Be certain to eat, before you dive into Maggie's treats."

"We can catch up on the highlights from Denver in a minute," Maggie slid into the chair beside Tory. "What was Ginny talking about? What are you worrying over?"

Tory explained the rescue, the petition, and the Equine Advocates request for her to bid for public sympathy at the fair. "Sounds like you do have it figured out. Now give me the Denver highlights. I want to hear it all but I only have time for the cliff notes. Believe it or not, I have a flesh and blood date to the Sunday matinee."

Tory panicked, "Not a cyber flirt, I hope."

"No," Maggie giggled. "Mike from the hardware store."

"He's married," Tory scolded.

"I'm aware of that, as is his very pregnant wife." Maggie laughter bubbled. "He wanted to take the twins to see the new Disney movie. I'm an extra pair of hands."

"Oh."

"You should come." Maggie bounced toward the door.

"Oh," Tory repeated with alarm. "No thanks. I've scarier business to take care of. I'll leave controlling four-year-olds in a public place to you."

Tory sat alone in the quiet kitchen for another twenty minutes. No matter how she tried there wasn't a better answer. Sodden with surrender she eased her phone from her pocket, flipped open the device, punched a few buttons.

Remi placed her head in Tory's lap. "Time to make Lauren's day," Tory stroked absently as she waited for the call to connect to the president of the Equine Advocacy.

The squeal of delight was still ringing in Tory's head. She lowered her cheek against Remi's soft fur. "Lauren's happy," Remi's tail thumped. "You're happy too," Tory chuckled. "I, on the other hand, am unhappy. Aside from suffering irreparable damage to my inner ear, I just agreed to go to the fair."

CHAPTER TWENTY

Tory's mood needed a tangible and positive hour. Ariel was healing well and growing more confident. Tory took her time brushing her body, detangling her mane and tail. The horse relaxed as Tory soothed with touch and voice. Hands replaced tools. Tory applied pressure over the rigid tissue, releasing toxins, and lessening scar tissue.

Therapy complete, Tory led the mare to the indoor arena. She snapped a lunge line to the halter and circled Ariel at a slow pace. The movement encouraged the muscles in her hips and legs to extend and flex.

"She's looking fantastic." Dale entered the arena.

"I agree." Tory reeled her in. "Think I will try to saddle her tomorrow. Not ride," she hurried to say. "I have no history so I don't know what ability she has. Hate to foster her out as a pasture buddy if she's hiding talents."

Dale leaned over the rail. Ariel bumped his arm with her nose. "Looking for your treat?" Dale reached in his pocket and offered a carrot.

"Would you mind returning her to the paddock?"

"Always my pleasure to walk a lady home."

Tory gathered the caddy of grooming supplies and headed toward the main barn, dogs on her heels. She reached for the stable door and shrieked as it thrust open in front of her.

Avery's lips quirked, "Sorry about that." He knew checking in on Peach and Titan was the responsible thing to do. He hoped saving the task for the end of the day would increase his odds of running into Tory.

This morning he'd gone to her room with tea and aspirin, but discovered the maid service at work turning over the room.

Tory patted her chest to steady her scrambling pulse. "Hi."

Avery found himself absorbing the beauty that was Tory Keen. Swallowed in an oversized jacket, hair restrained beneath a multicolor knitted hat, "Nice beanie."

She pulled the cap from her head scattering her hair like wildfire across her shoulders.

"My Nana made this. Each is one is unique and one of a kind." Her voice spiked, "You'd be lucky to own one."

Tory thrust by him and placed the grooming tote on the shelf. Where on Earth had the temper shot from? Shame scorched her cheeks.

"I wasn't trying to upset you," Avery said quietly.

Keeping her back to him she whispered. "For some odd reason it takes you little effort to ruffle me." Her cell phone rang, she answered. "Tory Keen."

"Hello Miss Keen, we met yesterday."

The suit. Her day was getting better and better. "Grey Stone Plantation."

"Correct. The first leg of the Triple Crown is approaching, and we were hoping…"

His voice buzzed like a swarming hive inside her skull. Compensation quotes, travel expenses, private accommodations and meal allowance. He was as persistent and persuasive as he'd been over dinner in Denver.

Tory decided her fatigue weakened brain was to blame as she conceded every proposed point. With a curse she snapped the phone closed, then frowned when the alert sounded. She opened the email and read confirmation of her flight and trip itinerary. For the second time in an hour Tory felt bulldozed. She placed fisted hands on hips and released a weary breath.

"You said yes."

Tory startled, flushed under Avery's scrutiny. She'd forgotten he was there. He made her feel so unsteady, so aware. "Yeah, looks like I may need to buy a ridiculous hat."

Frustrated strides carried her toward the house, dogs nipping at her heels. In her wake, flurries blew through the open stable door. A horse whinnied, another nickered, Avery's heart thumped hard in his chest.

He pushed the door closed.

CHAPTER TWENTY-ONE

Tory nibbled on a blueberry muffin and was contemplating a chocolate croissant when she heard knuckles rap at the back door. Poncho and Remi barked excitedly as Avery stepped into the mudroom. Tory felt worse about snapping at him than the calories she was punishing herself with.

"Step out of your boots, and I'll treat you to a hot drink and a buffet of pastry."

"I need to head back to town," Avery said.

"I can't apologize if you don't come inside for a moment. Maggie dumped all of these baked delicacies on my counter and if you can't spare me the time to make amends I'll stand rooted right here and shove each and every last one into my mouth."

"That would be something to watch."

"So would the sight of me bent over the porch rail retching it all back up."

"Nice image." Avery chuckled.

"Just a minute or two?" Tory pleaded. "The house is empty and quiet. The snow is blanketing. Pick a treat and visit with me?"

Avery looked intently at her for a long moment. Her heavy hair casually braided hung across the shoulder of her rag wool sweater. Silly printed pajama pants ended at mismatched fleece socks. He should move along, for exactly the same reasons she wanted him to stay.

Deep within the home a clock chimed. The lonely tones echoed off plaster, stone, and wood. Avery pulled off his gloves and slid the zipper of his coat down. He eyed the counter burdened with baked goods. "Where did your friend find all of these?"

"Find? You're kidding." Tory laid a napkin on the counter. "Made. Maggie makes the best baked goods in all the land." She gestured to the treats. "Help yourself. Hot tea, coffee, cocoa?"

Avery selected a double chocolate chunk cupcake, "Whatever you're having."

"Cocoa." Tory settled a saucepan on the burner, poured in cold milk.

His teeth sank in. "Holy cow, this is amazing."

"As I said," Tory waved her hand in a broad circle. "Maggie is the best in all the land." Absently she stirred and added cocoa powder and sugar. "I guess I owe you two apologies. First, for my over-indulgence at the conference. Must have been fun dumping an inebriated woman in her hotel room. Second, tonight's bad temper. I made a decision to panhandle at the fair." Her shoulders lifted and fell. "Sorry times two."

"As to Denver, I liked seeing you relax. I enjoyed delivering you to your room. I'm only sorry I didn't get to take you to breakfast before your flight."

Tory smiled and offered a mug with mini-marshmallows bobbing on the surface.

"Homemade, nice. How's cottage living?"

"Peaceful, and clean. That will change tomorrow."

"Your brother," Avery paused.

"Murphy," Tory supplied.

"Right, and his wife and son."

"Good with the details," Tory beamed. "Jess and Riley."

"The birthday boy. You'll be grateful for your own space when they're all here, don't you think?'

"I will admit, I enjoyed the silence for the first few days. But I'll like knowing someone's nearby." Tory trailed off sipping her warm chocolate.

"You love it," Avery finished.

"I do. I always wanted a big family. When we relocated here it was bam... instant family. Grandparents, ranch hands, their spouses and kids, no shortage of love. It was a wonderful transition for Murphy and me. We were so busy making new friends our hearts were mended before we knew it." Tory smiled, "My mom regained her footing and met Ed. They're married now and love to travel."

"Where's your father?" Avery asked.

She shrugged, "Not here."

"Sorry, that was rude."

"You're quick to apologize. Your mom did a good job on you." She picked up her phone. "What's her number? I need to congratulate her."

Avery smiled, "She's a great woman, a lot like your mom, I figure."

Tory lifted a brow. "Have you met my mother?"

"Nope but I'm thinking they're kindred, my mom and yours. Making something better from the unexpected," he explained.

Tory studied him over the rim of her mug. She recognized the scars of divorce. Wishing to erase the cloud of sadness, Tory nudged the treats toward him. "Tell me about your mom."

Avery selected a fruit filled croissant. "She worked three jobs and fed me, clothed me, and made certain I worked to my potential in school." Avery shook his head. "I have no idea how she managed it or where she found the time or cleverness to make it appear simple. We were a team, still are." He smiled now. "She'd kill for a peek at the recipes for these muffins."

"Maggie guards her secrets more fiercely than Ginny."

Avery's cell phone buzzed at his hip. "Her ears must be burning. Excuse me a moment," – "Hi Mom."

Tory stepped to the sink, rinsed the mugs, and placed them in the dishwasher. She smiled when Avery laughed at something his mother said.

The similarities in their childhood explained Tory's ease in connecting to the boy he was. His laid-back warmth paired with his proven competence in the stables made her acutely aware of her desire to connect with the man.

Avery strolled in, reclined against the counter. "Mom is watching the weather network. She said they're reporting record snowfalls for our area."

"Anything over an inch is a record to a thin skinned resident of the East Coast." Tory laughed. "Stick around, you'll toughen up. I- I-mean," she stammered. "If you'd done this rotation first, you'd have experienced serious winter weather." She removed the plastic container from the cupboard.

Avery observed Tory's nervous energy as she sorted through the pastries. She snapped the lid closed, grabbed a roll of tape from a drawer, and fastened a card to the cover. With a bright smile she pushed the filled Tupperware toward him.

"What's this?"

"I'm marketing Maggie's baked goods. Her number's on the top." Tory tapped her finger to the business card. "Tell your mom about the ones you like best. Let her work on Maggie and see if she can wrangle a secret or two." Tory leaned an elbow on the bar.

"I bet she wheedles a few." Avery pulled on his parka. "Thanks for the cocoa and the treats." As he lifted the box their eyes met and held.

"You're welcome." She noted the flash of awareness brightening his blue eyes. Tory looked at the floor, shifted her feet. "I have a murky memory of our first kiss. I'm not reckless or casual despite the impression I may have given in Denver." Warmth spread in the pit of her stomach. She cocked her head, and with the plastic container as a buffer, leaned in and brushed a feather light kiss over his cheek.

Avery weighed the fallout of initiating a second more satisfying kiss. He had a feeling when he dove in, he'd want to stay under. He placed the pastry down and tilted toward her. "I know things are crazy in your world and are about to get even more so, but could we maybe squeeze in a dinner?"

Tory's heart surged. "I'd like that."

"When?"

"Oh...well," She laughed. "I haven't a clue."

Avery reached out, snagged her pinkie between his thumb and index finger. "Okay, how about this? I'm interested in finding time to get to know you better."

"I'm interested in making the time to get to know you too."

He lifted her hand to his lips, placed a chaste kiss on her knuckles. "Goodnight, Tory." In the mudroom, Avery paused before opening the door to the blustery cold. He tapped the top of the container and grinned. "Thanks for the treats."

CHAPTER TWENTY-TWO

The hot shower felt like heaven. Avery rubbed the towel roughly over his head then secured the plush terry around his hips. His mind was full of Tory Keen. A contradiction at every turn, tough and tender, smart and sassy. On impulse he snagged his phone and dialed her number.

"Keen residence."

"Tory, it's Avery. What are you doing?"

"Settling in for a Sunday night movie with the dogs."

"Anything worth braving the storm?"

Tory's belly flipped, "You just left."

"Doc Webb left me a couple of cool toys, a snow mobile and a four-wheeler. I figure if I want the full Montana veterinary experience, I should see what an emergency call looks like in the winter. Not the most traditional date, I realize."

"Why spend the money on dinner and a movie, if a cup of coffee will answer the same question?"

"What?"

"Just something I read in a women's magazine," Tory sighed. "People spend a fortune trying to get to know one another. The average first date can run a hundred dollars, and you never learn anything about anyone while you're chomping down over-priced entrees. Or a movie date, for example, two hours of zero conversation in a pitch-black theater. You've dropped major change and barely scratched the surface on whether or not you want to spend more time together. It's crazy."

"When you put it that way," Avery took a deep breath. "Let's see, we've done birth, breakfast, moved furniture...We've covered hotel bars, pastry and cocoa... I think I'm ready for a traditional date,"

Avery chuckled. "Not that I'm entirely sure picking you up on an ATV would classify as conventional."

Tory lifted the curtain and looked at the light over the stable door. Steady plump snowflakes dropped. "The snow's really coming down, Avery."

"Now you sound like my mom. They're calling for eight inches and we already have six. I say it's only going to get better."

Her hand pressed to her nervous middle. "Well in the name of career research I guess you could head over."

Avery reveled at her dry tone.

Tory heard the click in her ear and her heart fluttered. She walked to the base of the steps, and punched the speed dial for Maggie.

"Hey girl, got the snowed-in blues?"

"Actually, I'm getting company."

"What company?" It only took a moment for Maggie to clue in, "Ohhhhh, sexy vet?"

Tory's nerves amped higher. "What in the world am I thinking?"

"Who gives a rat's tuckous?" Maggie snickered. "Live it up. What are you wearing?"

"My jammies."

"Well as appealing as cartoon-printed flannel might be, I suggest your bootcut jeans and the sinfully luxurious cashmere sweater Murphy gave you for your birthday."

"We're going for a four-wheeler ride, I can't wear cashmere."

"You most certainly can. Now change your clothes, and Tory? Don't behave." Maggie cackled, "I'll call in the morning for details."

Tory raced up the wooden steps. A chance at living out the stories written across the pages of the novels she loved. The first date... "Pressure." Tory laughed, "If only Nora Roberts would pen the next few pages for me." She chuckled at herself then squeaked when she saw the clock. She shucked her pajamas and whipped open her closet door. Deciding Maggie did know best Tory tugged the plum colored sweater over her head.

Tory clutched Avery's jacket, "You're crazy!" she threw her head back and squealed as he whipped the four-wheeler into a tight turn, showering the field with flying snow.

He raced along the stream and across the meadow, then slowed and allowed the machine to drift to a stop.

"Everything okay?" Tory asked.

He cut the engine, "It's beautiful." The mountains jutted into the brilliant star speckled sky. The moonbeams reflected making the snow glisten like tinsel on a fir tree at Christmas. "No city lights or traffic to mar the night, only dark and quiet. My first night in the apartment at Doc Webb's I thought something was wrong. When I looked outside my window I could see where the light, cast from the dusk-to-dawn light, met the edge of black in a hush that was more unsettling than the darkness. It took me awhile to figure out the source of my anxiety."

"What was it?" Tory asked curiously.

"Nothing," he laughed, "total, absolute, stillness."

"It's a wondrous thing."

"You said you and Murphy came out west when you were young, right?"

"We did," Tory climbed from the seat and stretched. "My mother brought us to the ranch. My grandparents were special people, they gave us a new life. My grandpa, oh, what a character he was..." she trailed off lost in a memory. "He had the heart of a mischievous teen, and my Nana was smart as a whip with a wicked sense of humor. They loved each other so much, and it showed in everything they touched."

"Sorry you've lost them."

"I still can picture them snuggled up by the fire or bickering in the kitchen." She trailed off on a wistful breath. She walked a few feet away. The snow packed beneath her feet. "They showed Murphy and me the rewards of ranching, while encouraging us to chase our own interests. It was a daily joy for them, not work. But above everything else, they believed the open range offered the opportunity for complete clarity." She turned toward him. "Heavy stuff for a first date, Doc."

"I guess it is."

"How are you finding life beyond the Mississippi?"

"I was looking for an adventure before I settled in Maryland. Meeting Doc Webb and listening to his passion for Montana made me curious. It didn't hurt that he saw a quality in me that made him want to potentially pass his practice on to me." He laughed, "Like I said before, the open bar helped. My Mom encouraged me to give it a shot. 'It's only a few weeks of your life,' she said, 'Go see if it fits'."

"Does it?" Tory felt the heat crawl across her cheeks and was grateful for the scarf tied over her face. "Directness, it's a curse." She dipped her head, walked back to the ATV, and leaned against the seat.

"The caseload has been intense, and you're right, I missed a true winter." He nudged the four-wheeler with his boot. "If cruising to a ranch on a motorized toy is what I could look forward to, well then," His eyes lit with boyhood merriment. "What's your favorite season, Tory?"

"Spring," she said without hesitation. "Springtime on Keen Ranch is my favorite. Babies of all varieties, wildflowers blooming across impossibly green meadows, melting snow, swollen streams, and snow tipped mountains for the backdrop. Definitely Spring."

He could picture Tory skipping through the tall grass with crimson pigtails flying, and a bunch of wildflowers clutched in her fist. "You're happy here? No pangs for busy suburban life?"

"Houses on top of houses, public schools, mass transit, and the gambit of urban hustle bustle? No. I expected I would, as I got older. My obsession with women's magazines keeps me in the loop," she smiled. "I miss Joel, that's for sure, but technology lessens the vacancy. If only I could get him out here for an entire year, I know he'd stay forever."

A thoughtful gleam flooded Tory's brown eyes. Avery banked the glint of green which prodded him to inquire more about this 'Joel' person.

Avery's gaze was so intent, Tory fought the urge to look away. "I enjoy the brushes I get with suburbia from time to time when I speak at or attend conferences, but no, I don't long for life in the city."

"One more question before I lose my head and kiss you. Are you dreaming of a solo trip around the world, or a third world humanitarian outreach that takes you out of the country for years."

Tory failed to hear another word beyond 'kiss you'. She stared up into Avery's strong face, "You want to?"

"Someday, maybe."

Tory's eyebrow crinkled in confusion. "Huh?"

"Go to a third world country? I'd appreciate the adventure."

The night concealed her flush. It was obvious she'd misheard him.

Avery stepped closer, and crouched in front of her. "Tory, what did you think I said?"

Why had she chosen this moment to daydream? Tory squared her shoulders, thrust her chin high. "I thought you said you were going to kiss me."

Insecurity wavered in her eyes in direct contrast with her bold posture. "I did." Avery reached out and laid his gloved hands over hers. "Like you, I try not to be reckless or casual."

Her unease floated away like a helium balloon and was replaced with a bubbling thrill. Tory took a calming breath. "Okay."

"Okay?" he chuckled and tugged until they were both standing. "Should I pass you a note?"

"What would your note say?"

Avery smiled, "Will you be my girlfriend?"

Tory shook her head from side to side, and enjoyed the quick flash of disappointment on his face. "Too fast, how about – Do you like me?" She giggled now, "Yes or no."

"I'm out of practice," Avery chuckled. "Yes."

"And then I would pass a note back that asked – Do you want to kiss me?"

"We've covered that, on my side anyway. So, at great risk of being caught by the teacher, I would pass the paper back again and ask you – Do you want to kiss me?"

"Yes," Tory said so quietly he nearly missed it.

He pulled off his gloves, reached up to her scarf covered face. Gently he eased the crocheted material down. "Nana make this too?" Tory could only nod. She was bundled in inches of downy layers but as he undressed her face she felt naked…exposed.

Avery knew she was beautiful, but in this setting she radiated. Her amber eyes were trained on his, her breath released in white bursts. Deliciously unhurried, he framed her cold cheeks in his warm hands. The sigh that slipped from her lips was the sweetest music.

Tory's eyes fluttered closed. Her heart thundered in her chest. She wondered if anything could match the expectation of a simple brush of lips.

"Not our first but…" he whispered as he traced his thumb along her jaw, easing up and over her unpainted bottom lip. "What are you doing to me?"

The lids that had fallen snapped open. Avery was inches away. Focused intently on her. She was about to tell him she wasn't doing anything when he silenced her, most effectively, by capturing her mouth with his.

A jolt surged through her. She leaned closer and pressed against him. She had been kissed before, Tory thought absently, but good heavens did Avery know his business.

Together they sank until they were kneeling in the soft cushion of snow. His hands left her face, his fingertips feathered across her cheeks and dove into her mass of hair. Nerve endings on her scalp leapt to life, stoking the furnace rooted deep inside her.

Avery eased back and brushed her hair off her shoulder. "You ready to head back?" He pushed to his feet then held his hands out to pull her up.

Tory blinked. Of all the things she expected to follow a mind numbing kiss, being asked politely to head home wasn't one of them.

Avery pulled his gloves on and straddled the machine. The engine roared to life. Tory replaced the scarf, regained her seat, and wrapped her arms around Avery a second before the unit shot across the meadow.

By the time they had reached the house Tory had rehearsed five easy ways to escape further humiliation and end the evening. It was obvious their kiss hadn't had the same effect on Avery. *Cut your losses*, she chastised herself.

The dogs raced in circles around the noisy machine barking their welcome. Avery pulled to the rear of the house and shut down the motor. "Hey Remi, Poncho," he said easily. "What's the schedule for the movie portion of our evening?" Poncho leapt into Avery's lap and licked his goggles. "Hey, no necking until the final credits."

Tory climbed off the ATV. Remi sat obediently in the snow, tail wagging. "There's my mannered lady," Tory rubbed the old girl's head. "It's frustrating that you can't teach Poncho proper behavior."

Avery extracted himself from the young dog and stood.

Tory studied him as he took off his gloves and hat and unzipped his coat. "You really want to stay for a movie?"

Avery brows crinkled, "Did I lose my invite?"

Tory shook her head even as the confusion swirled. Maybe he's lonely and she was the only friend he'd made. Friends, she wanted to groan. A closeness born in tragedy was doomed. They'd be forever bonded by sadness.

Avery touched her sleeve, "You in there?" He stared into Tory's vacant eyes. "Your brain is chewing on something. What's worrying you?"

"Straight talk?"

"You said it's your thing," Avery crossed his arms over his chest. "Let's have it."

"Impromptu date, snowmobile ride, gorgeous scenery and a whopper kiss followed by a fast exit, a platonic ride back, playful dogs, and a movie invite."

"So?" Avery was genuinely baffled.

"Are we destined to be friends because we met under extreme circumstances?"

Avery let out a bemused breath. "How many of these women's magazines do you read?"

"You said straight talk."

"I'd hate to hear curved." Avery scrubbed a hand over his chin, "Let me try to follow your logic. We met during a sad, stressful situation; we liked each other enough to drink a few cocktails and eat some pastry. We enjoyed a ride with spectacular scenery, shared a spontaneous kiss, which I ended with the hope I could talk you into a soft couch, hot fire, and a mood setting movie."

Liking his interpretation better then hers, Tory tossed up her hands. "Feeling a bit like an idiot."

"Don't," Avery grabbed her hand and pulled her toward her cottage. "But, could we get to the fire? I hate to blow my macho, but I'm freezing."

Avery laughed heartily, as Reese Witherspoon's fist plowed into the face of her would be mother-in-law. He had never seen *Sweet Home Alabama*. Tory had told him it was a hoot, and she had been right. The sappy ending had Tory swooning as the destined couple finally embraced beneath a bolt of lightning.

"True love makes the heart go pitty pat." Tory tossed the throw over the back of the couch. "What'd you think?" She carried the empty popcorn bowl to the kitchen a few steps away. Avery followed her with the drink glasses. He rinsed and placed them on the top shelf of the dishwasher.

The kitchen was cozy, a fact Tory liked in theory. She hadn't given much thought to maneuvering around another person. Especially a hard lean specimen like the hunk behind her.

Avery turned quickly, his hip caught Tory, "Sorry."

"No problem. I was just thinking I could use another foot or two of wiggle room in the kitchen. Renovation plans were made thinking one person, not company. Did you like the movie?" Tory skirted the counter, opened the door for the dogs.

"I liked it a lot." Avery moved behind her and watched the dogs racing in circles in the snow. He rested his hands on her shoulders. "The credits are rolling," his head dipped and he laid his lips on the side of her neck. "Do I have to pass you a note?"

She could feel the heat of his body against hers. Tory turned and captured his mouth. Prepared for the punch of heat, she welcomed it, and chased more.

Avery's hands trailed along her spine and back up again. Poncho returned and scratched the door.

"Thin skinned beach puppy." Tory regretted breaking the circle of Avery's arms. She held the door open and the dogs raced past her to claim warm spots in front of the fire.

"Come on, Avery, bundle up, I'm kicking you out."

"Here's your hat and don't let the door…"

"No, you don't," she wagged her finger. "You won't muddle our first date with slang phrases and dirty talk."

"Dirty talk?" he chuckled, "there's an idea." Her woolen sock covered feet shifted nervously. He stepped closer and took her hands into his. Strong but delicate hands, he thought, as he looked at their fingers. "I think our inexpensive date went well. I'd like to have another."

"My brother comes home tomorrow. I'm flying to Kentucky the next day. When I get back I have to prepare for the fair." Tory shook her head and sighed, "Not sure how I get pulled in so many directions."

"Generosity seems to be your curse." His thumbs brushed slow circles over her knuckles. "Let's take one moment at a time." Avery gathered her close, rested his forehead against hers. "How about I make sure I bump into you tomorrow?"

She lifted her face, "I'll look forward to impact."

CHAPTER TWENTY-THREE

Tory replayed the conversation she'd had with Ginny and Dale over breakfast. They'd maneuvered around her, like snipers in the grass, while affably passing the eggs. Without a thought, Tory relinquished Murphy's flight information and waved Dale off wishing him safe travels to the airport.

Yes, she had a lot on her plate, but Murphy was *her* brother and *she* was the one responsible for meeting him at the terminal. "Ginny?" Tory hollered as she stomped through the breezeway.

The soundtrack to *Chicago* swirled in the kitchen. Ginny stood at the counter tearing hunks of dough and tossing them into a cake pan lined with chopped nuts. "Mind your fury, young one," she said easily as Tory burst into the room. "There's not a reason in the world for your feet to pound those newly laid planks. They didn't do a thing to you."

"Ginny," Tory tried for stern but the fragrance wafting from the saucepan – melted butter, sugar, and a secret concoction of cinnamon spiced sweetness – weakened her resolve.

Ginny wrapped the handle with a towel and poured the simmering blend over the uncooked bread. Her sticky buns would be the perfect treat for the travelers. "What's bothering you, Tory love?" Ginny covered the pan then moved to the sink to scrub potatoes for the welcome home feast.

"Do not 'Tory love' me. You and Dale worked me over, didn't you?"

"So what if we did?" Ginny hummed a bar of *All that Jazz*.

Tory gasped, "You're not even going to deny it?"

"What would be the point in that?" Ginny wiped her hands on her apron. "You need to ready the house. You have children coming for lessons and responsibilities in the stables. You can't do a half a dozen tasks one hundred percent well. Dale and I just took one chore off your list, is all. No harm."

"You worked me over," Tory pouted. "I don't care for it."

"Noted."

Ginny's' quick agreement riled Tory even more. She shoved the irritated haze far enough away to notice a ghost of a smile and a quiet unshed tear tipping Ginny's lashes. Tory stepped to the stove and wrapped arms around Ginny's middle. "It's just the thing Nana would have done for me. I love you."

"Grab me a tissue, girl," Ginny sniffed. "I love you and Murphy like you're my very own. In a couple of hours this house will be bursting the way I like it best, with family." Ginny heaved a sigh, "A few months ago I would have told you my heart was filled to the top. But Jess and Riley..." Ginny removed her glasses, patted the gentle weeping. "They just shoved right in and made themselves cozy, didn't they?" She blew her nose and washed her hands.

Tory laughed lightly and handed Ginny a towel. "Never thought I'd see Murphy so settled. He sure got the whole package." Tory wondered if she'd ever be so lucky.

"You'll find the same when the time is right."

"What?" Tory sneered, "I'm not jealous."

"Of course not, jealous is an ugly word but you do want a family of your own, right?"

"Someday..." Tory trailed off.

Ginny had hoped she'd be able to see both Murphy and Tory married off and popping out babies. Wasn't until recently she thought she might get her wish. "I'm going to set up the dining room table since we're going to have a crowd. It will be like the holidays minus Joel, I guess."

"We could put a cardboard cutout in his chair so the table will be full," Tory joked and kissed Ginny's cheek.

The morning passed in a blur of linens and final touches. The house was polished and tidy. The only thing missing was her family.

The sound of the dogs barking had Tory racing to the nearest window and lifting the curtain. Her heart fluttered when she spotted Avery's truck. "I'm running out to the barn."

"Tell Avery hello," Ginny lifted her voice, "and encourage him to bring his appetite as well as his good looks to my table."

Tory pulled a knit hat over her braid, "If I bump into him."

"Be a wasted trip if you don't soak up the sight of that fine piece of man."

"Really, Ginny," she ducked her chin to conceal her smile.

"Hush, I'm visualizing." The door slammed. Ginny picked up the paring knife and the tune playing in the kitchen. *Avery*, she mused. Her heart could be encouraged to make room for another.

The wind raced down the mountainside and across the open plains to slap at Tory's cheeks. She hurried toward the stable and opened the sliding door just enough to slip inside. Maggie was at the far end of the barn grooming Murphy's massive quarter horse. "Hey, how long you been here?"

"An hour or so," Maggie ran the soft brush over Kai's shoulder and down the length of his strong leg. "I decided to get the date details in person," Maggie snickered. "I poked my head in the kitchen, and Ginny said you were neck deep scrubbing. Got it all ready?"

"As it can be." Tory stepped in front of Kai and let him nuzzle her jacket. "Your master's coming home. I'll bet big money he takes you for a ride."

"Exactly what I thought, after two weeks without a saddle under him, Murphy will take him out no matter the weather. I plan to groom Bo and Babe in case the entire family wants to go."

"That's awfully nice of you, Maggie."

"I know, I'm a gem, now spill. Last night, date with Avery, and don't leave anything out."

Tory lowered onto a bale of straw. "I fed him pastry, we went for a ride in the snow, watched a..." Tory trailed off as the man in question strolled into view. His head was down and he was speaking into a recorder about medicine dosage and health updates. She swallowed and realized she had no idea what she'd been saying. Shaking her head clear her eyes returned to Maggie, "Ummm ahh yeah well..."

"Exactly." Maggie's grin was swift and depraved. "Hot men have that same effect on me."

Tory drew a breath and prepared to argue but Maggie's playful laugh stopped her. "Yummy, right?"

"Oh honey, yummy doesn't quite cover it. Is he coming to dinner?"

"I'm supposed to ask."

"Insist. I like visual appetizers."

Tory flicked Maggie's hip then hugged her. "I promise we'll have a girl's night soon."

She left Maggie to her work, and tried for a casual stroll toward Peach's stall.

"Hey," Avery looked up. "Your brother and his entourage make it home?"

"Not yet, Dale went to pick them up so I could do house stuff."

"Your list all marked off?"

"Yes," she leaned over the half door. "How's everyone feeling today?"

"These two are the poster children for orphan and nurse mare. As to your others, I think we're in for a busy night. Two mares in pre-labor and another who is thinking hard on the subject."

"Good thing I'm here to invite you to dinner."

"It's a family night, Tory."

"Well yes, but you want all the experience you can pack into your internship right? Ginny always sets an extra plate, and she said to bring your appetite." Tory omitted the other request. "If you leave the seat empty, you'll hurt her feelings."

"No pressure," he laughed and startled Titan.

"Straight talk?" Tory shifted to the side so Avery could pass. "I'd like you to join us."

Avery definitely wanted more time with Tory, and he wasn't fool enough to turn down a home cooked meal. "Sounds great."

CHAPTER TWENTY-FOUR

The welcome home dinner didn't quite work out the way it was planned. Dale pulled into the ranch with Murphy and family, barely set the parking brake before racing to the barn to see a chestnut filly drop into the world. It was an easy delivery for the four-year-old mare. Avery maneuvered from one stall and directly into the next. Jess and Riley made it in time for the second miracle to arrive.

Dinner had gone cold, but nobody seemed to mind.

Freshly showered, the labor and delivery crew gathered noisily around the maple dining room table. Murphy sat at the head with Jess and Riley on either side. Maggie, Avery, Dale, and Tory held the center, with Ginny anchoring the opposite end.

"Too much food, Ginny," Murphy teased, "But don't you worry, I'll eat an extra share."

"Don't think I won't hold you to it," Ginny placed her napkin on her lap. "We missed you, but now you're home with your lovely family."

"We're starving here," Dale complained, "Gush over them during dinner."

Ginny lowered her eyes, "I'm a silly old gal."

Murphy rose from his chair and kneeled at Ginny's side. "It's nice to be home." He pressed his cheek into her lap. "It's nicer to have been missed."

The move clutched Ginny's heart. She laid her weathered palm over Murphy's hair. "Say the blessing, will you, sweetie?"

They attacked her meal like warriors following a fierce battle. It pleased Ginny greatly to hear spoons clattering against the pottery as the last of the veggies were scooped out.

Tales of the Disney vacation bubbled with stories from the missed days on the ranch. Maggie shared the details of her latest venture into creative baking.

"Conversation Jacuzzi," Dale chuckled and winked at Ginny. "Balm for the soul, huh darlin'?"

With Jess's hand linked in his, Murphy observed another conversation unfolding without a single syllable. His wife tugged and raised her brow. Murphy dipped his head toward Avery and Tory. His frown deepened, "Something's going on there."

"Yep," Jess wiggled her fingers until Murphy's eyes connected with hers. "And you're going to stay out of it."

It was nearing ten o'clock when the group began to show signs of wear. The men left the kitchen to check on the new foals, and settle the livestock for the night. The table was cleared and the dishwasher hummed. Ginny gave the counter one final swipe with her dishrag then untied her apron.

Tory eyed the dessert, "Damn Maggie's oven and creativity."

"Yeah we should be wise and save them until tomorrow." Jess popped open the lid and groaned at the sight of countless pastries. "They'll be great for breakfast,"

"Mmm, I agree," Ginny opened the drawer and pulled out three clean forks. "But, I'd rather not toss and turn all night with visions of flaky, fruit-filled baked goods taunting me. Pick one, girls." Ginny filled the copper kettle with water, "We'll each have a bite or two and without a doubt, we'll sleep like babies. "Tea or coffee? We have Jamaican and Columbian."

"I love that your mom travels," Jess giggled. "Not that she isn't missed. The constant selection of the finest coffee in the world makes your kitchen seem like the posh coffee bar."

Tory nudged Ginny, "And Mom is away about forty-eight weeks a year."

"Not what I meant." Jess lifted her hands, "Decaf please, I'd actually like to sleep tonight."

"Mom?" Riley raced into the room and skidded to a halt, "Wow, is that dessert?" He licked his lips.

Jess moaned knowing it would be difficult to discourage him from eating the entire table of treats.

"Don't worry," Riley resisted the fare and jammed his hands in his pockets. "I want something better than sugar."

Jess scrutinized her energetic son, "You have my attention."

"Maggie told me she groomed Babe, Bo, and Kai. Can we go for a midnight family ride?"

Hard as it was for Jess to look in her little boy's face and disappoint him, she needed to do just that.

"Awww man," Riley read the 'no' in his mother's eyes.

Tory laid her hands on Riley's shoulders, "I could take him."

"Aunt Tory, you rock."

Riley raced from the room. Jess yelled after him, "Warm clothes, layers, we're not in Florida anymore." Jess shook her head at Tory, "You're crazy."

"It's a gorgeous night."

"Even still, you're traveling tomorrow."

"Not until midday. Why don't you and Murphy put the moon to good use, unless you're honeymooned out."

"Not possible." Murphy closed the door behind him, hung his coat on the peg. "What did I miss?"

"Your crazy sister is taking Riley for a ride. Now."

"Perfect night for it," Murphy skirted the counter and wrapped his arms around his wife. "Need help saddling?" He swept Jess off her feet and cradled her in his arms, "Or may we say goodnight?"

Jess protested without conviction as he strode from the room then called out, "Goodnight."

Ginny laid her palm over her heart, "Better than one hundred pages of a Nicholas Sparks best seller."

Tory agreed. The love between her brother and Jess was achingly sweet.

Ginny poured decaf into her travel mug and wrapped an oversized blueberry muffin in a napkin, "And on that note, I'm off for home and my Sleep-Number bed. You and Riley stick close to home and ride safe."

CHAPTER TWENTY-FIVE

Elbow hinged over the top rail of the riding ring, Tory watched Riley atop Kai. The horse looked even bigger under his small form.

"Ask him to trot, Riley. Use your legs, squeeze." Kai's ears tipped back listening to the command. Understanding and obeying, the horse's pace quickened and Riley bounced lightly in the saddle.

Avery angled alongside Tory at the rail. Not touching, but close enough to give her heart rate a bump.

"Boy's got a solid seat."

"He's a fast learner," Tory smiled, "come summer we won't be able to hold him back."

"Can I go out and ride along the fence, Aunt Tory?"

"I'm not up for walking the fence tonight."

"Man…" he moaned.

"You're bumming him out, Aunt Tory," Avery muttered.

Riley circled Kai closer to the adults. "You could saddle up Bo. The moon's bright and the air's crisp. It's a beautiful night for a ride." He could sense her wavering and like a skilled hunter, he pressed his advantage. "I'll stick to the fence and turn back as soon as you tell me to. No whining, I promise, even if you cut us short."

Avery snickered, "Got quite the spiel going."

"You can come too, Avery," Riley said. "Maggie groomed Bo and Babe. Tack up and we can all enjoy a ride. Mom's always saying grab life and stuff. Isn't this one of those times?"

Tory released a weary breath, "Careful Avery, the kid's a slippery one.

The late night air and fatigue weighed heavily on Riley. His shoulders drooped in the saddle as they made the final turn toward the barn.

"Riley, ride Kai up to the back door," Tory eased Babe alongside her equine partner. "You're off the hook tonight."

"I'm not tired. I'll help cool them down, and put the gear away. I can do it." His words slurred.

"We've got it. You go in quietly, everyone will be sleeping. Strip off your coat and hang it up in the mudroom." She reached across, held the reins as he melted from the saddle to the ground. "Straight to your room, Riley, and crawl into your bed. I'll tuck you in just as soon as I tuck in the horses."

Tory rubbed the cloth across the saddles to remove any dust or dirt. Maintaining the equipment was as vital a routine as feeding the horses. Avery handed Tory the bridles. She stretched high, and hung them on the proper pegs.

Avery studied her. After the day they had weathered, she'd found the energy and compassion to take her nephew on a midnight ride. "You're pretty amazing, Tory Keen."

The surprise compliment brightened her face. She turned and smiled at Avery across the tack room. He looked so perfect leaning against the raw beam supporting the roof. Haunting five o'clock shadow mingled with the perfume of rawhide and oil...Tory's eyes made a leisurely trip from scarred leather boots to exquisitely strained denim, passing narrow hips, and a fleece sheathed chest, and returned to his face.

Avery's lips twitched.

Any thought of embarrassment left with reason, when his mouth bloomed into a wolfish grin. Tory leaned, the motion propelled her forward and her mouth locked on his. The world shifted beneath her feet. Her strong hands gripped muscled arms, and drew a wanton moan from an undiscovered depth. She closed the remaining few inches, and fused her long line of limbs tight against him.

Avery angled his head and took the kiss deeper. He groaned, banded his arms firmly around her and reversed their positions.

Tory felt the bite of the wood against her back. Avery's eyes, dark with controlled passion, burrowed into hers. Her body surged to life and quivered for more. She shivered and dove into another lingering kiss.

His lips left hers to cruise the line of her neck, and hovered over her thundering pulse. His nimble fingers opened the top few buttons of her shirt and allowed him to journey further until he nipped her collarbone. The catch of her breath thrilled him as he retraced the path and claimed her mouth once more.

He growled against her busy lips.

Her breath was clipped and ragged. Her cheeks flushed, tinting her porcelain skin with the most erotic shade of pink he'd ever seen. Avery's lips brushed her ear. "How about I grab my sleeping bag and we share the loft?"

Tory's hesitation was brief, but the flash of uncertainty was enough. Avery eased back to examine her face. Her eyes were closed, her cheeks chafed from the bite of his beard. Her lips lush and swollen were pressed together as if savoring the passion. The rise and fall of her chest drew his eyes to pale flesh tinted with the same blush that heated her neck.

Avery's gut clenched. Not reckless or casual but as the tide of hormones ebbed he'd put money on innocent. Gently, he closed her shirt, "I'm rushing you." Avery turned his back on Tory's bewildered expression, and rubbed his hand over his face in an effort to erase the desire she'd stirred.

The distance separating them felt greater than the few inches. Tory stepped toward him, wrapped her arms around and held tight. "Avery, …tell me what's wrong." She felt him tense. "Damn it," she thumped her hand on his shoulder. "Don't stop."

Avery laughed as her fevered temper lashed him as successfully as her seduction. He opened his arms and gathered her close. "You aren't...there's nothing …I just… shouldn't have..."

"Shouldn't have," hurt washed over her, obliterating excitement as effectively as a rush of water on loose sand. Her hands pressed against his chest as she tried to wiggle away. Avery's hold softened but he didn't release her. "Will you let me explain?" She eased back, dropped her head to his chest. She busied herself with securing the buttons on her shirt.

"Explain what exactly?" He stilled her fingers. "That you are virtuous enough to be selective?" Avery tucked her hair back and waited for her eyes now bright with tears to focus on his. "I could kick myself for assuming."

"What? That I'm a Montana hussy?" Tory snorted, "Quite the opposite. I'm just surprised you didn't get the Montana memo or spy the huge 'V' tattooed on my..."

"You have a tattoo?" Avery interrupted. "I would've discovered it sooner or later."

Tory relaxed against him, and sank into his body. "I'm a twenty-seven-year-old who knows what I'm asking for. You better be up for the challenge."

Avery laughed and tightened his arms, as the double meaning hit.

"Let go of me," Tory squirmed.

"Not a chance." In one swift motion Avery scooped her into his arms. He sat on the edge of the trunk with his lap full of woman. Not just any woman, Tory Keen. Jackpot.

Tory twisted until her upper body aligned with his. Avery gripped her waist stilling her movements. He brushed his lips over her temple, "Give me a moment, okay?"

Tory could feel the heat radiating from him. She could see the pulse hammering along his neck. Empowered she threaded her fingers in his hair and tipped his head back forcing him to see her. "I'm a grown woman," she lowered her lips to his thundering pulse. His quick intake of breath encouraged her. "I have been selective," she feathered a kiss over his brow, "but more importantly...I've waited." Her hands ran across his shoulders, her gaze held steady and confident, as she leaned, in aching degrees, until her lips settled on his.

The gentle kiss heated Avery's blood. She nibbled the line of his jaw then returned to his mouth, sinking in this time. His hands clenched her jean clad hips searching for an anchor in the madness, as Tory initiated another searing kiss.

He lifted her and settled her with a leg on either side of his. Resting on her knees, she hovered above him. Avery tipped his face as her curtain of hair surrounded them. "You are so beautiful," his hands framed her face and brought her mouth back to his. He feasted like a ravenous man. Lips, teeth, and tongue drove them within an inch of sanity. Avery angled his head and took all Tory offered.

Grateful the position limited the contact of her body against his, Avery's hands roamed over her back, and rested against her bottom. He gentled the kiss, and once again rested his forehead against hers. "May I walk you home, Miss Keen?"

Tory eased back and opened her palms on his chest. She reveled in the rise and fall, delighted in his breathlessness.

"Before you drag out some magazine article wisdom and overanalyze, let me assure you," he kissed the tip of her nose. "Walking you home is costing me."

They strolled, hand-in-hand, to the private entrance of her cottage. Avery rooted his boots to the welcome mat. He knew a single toe inside, and he'd stay until morning. Instead he kissed her within an inch of reason, then nudged her over the threshold and closed the door.

Tory leaned against the solid wood and listened for life to rumble into Avery's engine. She heard the crunch of gravel as the truck drove down the lane.

In his room, Riley snored face down. One leg in his jeans, the other splayed across the comforter. Tory removed the tangle of denim and covered him with the fleece throw boasting all of the Disney Kingdom's famous faces. Resting on the pillow, a breath away from kissing his master's cheek was Poncho. Tory petted the pup, then smoothed Riley's rumpled hair, and walked down the staircase.

The mantle clock chimed the midnight hour. The dwelling and its inhabitants slept around her. Tory clicked lights off, strolled through her glass breezeway, and into her cottage.

Tory tossed a final log into the fire. The flames licked and caught, flickered then glowed hot. She pressed her fingertips to still tingling lips. She closed her eyes and could feel Avery gripping her hips, anchoring them together. Her insides still quivered and sparked an ache which rivaled the raging embers in the belly of the woodstove.

She could be cozy in the loft with him right now if she had decided to be spontaneous.

Instead she walked to her room and stripped every inch of clothing, folded back the comforter, and slid beneath cool sheets. Tory didn't resist the image of Avery's fingers caressing her curves like the soft fabric.

She snickered and decided this was a level of naughtiness Maggie would approve of. She drifted off with thoughts of Avery's hands, lips, and body…. and the promise of more to come.

CHAPTER TWENTY-SIX

Tory rubbed her hands over her face and stretched. In the east, the overture of pink and gold prepared to present sun. She tugged on flannel pants and slipped on her moccasins. Today's agenda, breakfast with the family, pack for Kentucky, and catch a flight.

In her living room, Murphy agitated the coals, and placed a small log over the bed of heat. Tory watched as he blew gently and smoke began to rise. The bark of the wood caught, and tiny flames fanned over the surface.

Tory smiled at her brother's back, "Boy Scout."

Murphy grinned and tossed another log on the fire. He closed the protective grate. "With all the craziness last evening, I didn't get you to walk me through your summer house."

"It's always crazy here, Murphy."

Murphy eased his hip onto the arm of the sofa. "I'm sorry you feel like you have to vacate your childhood home. We can work it out, the house is plenty big."

"It is, and we could, but we won't. I'm excited to have a space of my own." Tory walked to the refrigerator. "The cottage is full of wonderful memories." She poured two glasses of orange juice, handed one to Murphy, and then ran her hand over the canning table. "I would like very much to give you a tour of my home."

Twenty minutes later, Tory led Murphy through the breezeway and into the magnificent perfume of Ginny's kitchen. "See, not a bad deal at all."

"Good morning, Tory love. The day you come to table late…" Ginny trailed off, her head tipped to the side as Murphy moseyed in behind his sister. "And dragging my tardy devil with you."

"How am I tardy if the food's not off the stove?"

"Well Murphy darling, unlike your sister, you never arrive early."

"Your 'darling devil' knows if he's early he'd have to help cook." Murphy kissed Ginny's cheek, "Smart is what I am." He stole a chunk of potatoes from the pan, "Perfect spring morning, can you smell it?"

"I can."

Tory grinned at the two of them as she fixed a cup of tea.

Riley's feet bounded down the wooden planks. Murphy winced. "I should teach him to ride the banister until everyone's awake."

Tory laughed, "Everyone's up."

"Jess isn't." Murphy's brow knitted as Riley burst into the room and flopped on the floor to pet the dogs.

Riley's hair jutted from his scalp at gravity defying angles. His pajama top boasted a graphic of Spiderman, while his bottoms claimed loyalty to Batman and ended three inches shy of bare feet. "My heavens, Ginny," Riley sighed, "that food smells like the angels prepared it for the Lord himself."

Ginny snickered.

"Morning, Aunt Tory," Riley clambered up beside Murphy. "Morning, Dad, can I have coffee?"

"Nope," Murphy kissed the top of his head.

"How about pancakes to go with those potatoes?"

"Chocolate chip?" Ginny asked, and saw the sparkle brighten the youngster's eyes. "Fetch them from the cupboard, and wash the dog off your hands."

"Spoiled," Murphy muttered as Riley scrambled to search the pantry.

"It's impossible not to spoil me." Riley tossed the bag of chips on the counter, and turned the water on to scrub. "I'm a darling young devil."

Murphy rolled his eyes, "When I get back from delivering Aunt Tory to the airport you are working with me all afternoon. We're going to relocate Ginny's plants, which is very important business. You mess it up, she won't be fixin' you anything special ever again."

Riley examined Ginny's wrinkled face set in stern lines.

She nodded, "Your Dad speaks the truth, Riley. My plants are my babies."

Tory could hardly find fault in the industry that was Grey Stone Plantation. Her accommodations rivaled a five-star resort. Her two-story bungalow home was outfitted with a catering kitchen and a Florida room overlooking the training track. The library hosted ceiling to floor reading options, which Tory coveted, and a stone fireplace large enough to stand in. There was a fully equipped home gym, and a private in-ground pool.

The horses, a tier above, were treated like members of the royal family. They endured routine body treatments, acupuncture, and reflexology sessions. Their stables gleamed. The training equipment was top of the line. Countless high-tech apparatus, many of which were prototypes, used to measure each breath, and muscle contraction of the thousand pound athletes.

Immersed in the intricate Grey Stone timetable, Tory found not a moment was wasted. She listened to training strategy over breakfast, and reviewed computerized analysis of respiration and stride during lunch. In the evening, deliberations over diet and workout were levered against the horse's potential earnings from winning, or placing, in the top three finishers at the Kentucky Derby.

She made the most of her allotted time with the magnificent stallion. Tory had been provided a list of suitable contact and interactions with the animal. She'd been issued a longer list of the unacceptable. When she was fortunate to get a rare unsupervised moment with her charge, she pressed her face against his brawny neck, and transferred as much love and tranquility possible.

After dinner on her second night, Tory lingered over a perfectly prepared vanilla latte. She listened as Grey Stone tacticians calculated the weeks leading to the Derby. Tory understood it was a business. She grasped the fine tuning of the profit margin even as she knew, in her core, it wasn't for her.

Tory thanked the owners for extending the opportunity, and recommended three alternative therapists.

The following morning, she boarded a plane for home.

CHAPTER TWENTY-SEVEN

"So, no Derby?" Maggie unzipped Tory's suitcase.

"Not this year," Tory unpacked a stack of clothes and moved to her closet.

Maggie cradled a pair of embossed leather pumps. "For a woman who detests shopping, you have the most incredible collection of foot fashion." She hooked a russet heel over the aluminum rail. "It's the worst injustice my feet being two sizes smaller than yours." Maggie fell across Tory's bed, "Would've been cool to sip Mint Juleps, and balance funky hats on our heads. The Kentucky Derby," she said wistfully, "bucket-list item number seventeen."

Tory snickered, "You added a few since last we talked about it."

"Well if you weren't jetting all over the world, we could hang out, eat cake and plot our dream voyages." Maggie rolled to her side, ran her hand over Tory's comforter. "Talk about fantasies, this bedroom ensemble is so beautiful. Admit it, you're glad I ripped off the tags?"

"Yes," Tory's face flushed.

"No need to be embarrassed."

"That's not it," she flopped on the bed, stretched out next to Maggie, wriggling until their faces were inches apart. Tory hugged the pillow to her chest. "Avery made my bed."

The shock rendered Maggie speechless.

Tory took the advantage and plowed on, "We slept in the barn, had a drunk night in Denver, I kissed him, there, and here..." She smothered her face with the pillow and garbled the tail end of her confession.

"Wait!" Maggie gasped, struggled for breath. "Hang on," she pushed up and ripped the plush pillow from Tory's grip. "I heard midnight make-out, and a mass of incoherent syllables." She bounced onto her knees and narrowed her eyes. "You little tart, I'm so proud." Maggie clambered to her feet and jumped like a child in an inflated party house. "I'm going to pretend I'm not miffed at you for keeping scandalous secrets." She flopped beside Tory. "Spill, and don't even think about leaving a single morsel out. I'm ravenous, feed me."

Maggie sighed and cried, giggled and clapped. Tory felt terrible she hadn't shared with her best friend sooner.

"If my calculations are correct," Maggie tapped her finger to her pursed lips, "bed making would have taken place a week ago. You've been busy. What do you have planned next, and how can I help?"

Tory strolled along the rescues, accepted a welcome home kiss from Smooch. Losing her shyness Ariel walked to the gate. The mare, hale and hearty, extended her neck, and tested Tory's coat pocket for something sweet. Tory stroked the long line of her head and found herself thinking of Avery. She'd drafted a quick text before her flight to let him know her trip had been cut short, but she'd chickened out before pushing send.

Tory laid the cube on the flat of her open palm. Ariel's soft muzzle snatched the treat. "I know," Tory whispered and combed her fingernails through the tuft of mane falling over Ariel's eyes. "It's bad Karma wishing for a reason to call the vet."

In the outer paddock, Peach walked to the fence. Trailing behind, Titan hopped on gangly legs and knobby knees. "Hey Mamma," Tory laughed as Peach pressed her nose against her hip. "Sorry, Ariel beat you to it. Spoiled rotten, the lot of you, and I'm responsible. How about I give you some exercise and a thorough grooming? You'll have the deluxe equestrian spa package – massage, grooming, foot treatment, and braided mane. Sounds good, right? Give you a break from Titan and a chance to stretch those long beautiful legs." Titan tossed his head and pawed the fresh straw. "You want pampered, too?" Titan backed bashfully behind Peach, "Ladies first, big guy."

"Shouldn't she have cucumber slices over her eyes, and be wrapped hoof to tail in a puffy white robe?"

Tory jolted at the sound of Avery's voice. She hadn't seen him since their romp in the tack room. She fixed an easy smile as Avery closed the distance. "You missed that part of the party. Although, I think I heard a camera click earlier. The equine paparazzi may have sent a sleeze-zoid photographer to capture our unsuspecting Peach in a vulnerable situation. They're probably posting the cucumber picture on Instagram as we speak." Peach bumped Tory's arm asking for her complete attention.

Only a few steps away from her, Avery didn't resist or hide his intent. "You're home a day early, lucky me." He closed the distance and laid his mouth against hers.

Her lids fluttered closed blocking out everything but the infusion of feelings. The bristle brush slipped from her fingertips and rattled to the floor. Off kilter, she gripped his sweatshirt, until he relinquished her lips. "What was that for?"

"Me," Avery tucked a stray copper tendril behind her ear and kissed her tenderly, "That one's for you."

"Oh..." Tory sighed.

"How was Kentucky?" Avery released her and bent to retrieve the brush.

She shrugged, "Disappointing but not unexpectedly so. How about I tell you over dinner?"

Surprise brightened his features, "Sounds great." He kissed her again. A light brush of lips which had Tory's heart skipping gleefully in her chest. "I checked Ariel a moment ago. Her leg is healing well."

"It is. Doc Webb will be pleased."

Avery nodded his head. "Speaking of Webb, the goats will be ready to be discharged when he gets home Saturday. He's hoping to talk you into moving the pair here to Keen Ranch for rehabilitation."

"I wasn't sure what kind of special needs they'd end up with. Frankly I'd thought it unlikely they'd survive at all."

"The amputations will make life challenging but not impossible. We might have to fit them with boots until their legs heal." Avery ran his hand over his face, "What Doc Webb was able to do for them, I'm in awe."

"I know," Tory squeezed his forearm, "he's really great."

"Wait until you meet the goats. They have fantastic personalities."

"I'll have Dale work on an enclosure."

"Great," Avery leaned close, and whispered, "Webb is planning to sweet talk you into keeping them permanently. Word is you're a softie."

"True."

"Where, and when, do you want me for dinner?"

"My place, anytime you finish up."

Chapter Twenty-Eight

In the small cottage kitchen, water was simmering. Onions, garlic, and herbs were chopped according to the Food Network's instructions, and a sauté pan sat poised at the ready. It was the first meal she'd prepared for an invited guest. Tory pressed a hand to her panicked belly. She'd selected a simple pasta, and spring mix salad.

Maggie and Jess stood at the counter, their conversation a faint hum on the edge of Tory's busy mind. Jess had mixed herbed butter, baked fresh multigrain bread. Maggie brought tiramisu and a bottle of wine. It should've been embarrassing, everyone knowing her business, but Tory found she didn't have the heart to complain.

At Maggie's insistence Tory wore an ankle length dress and killer red heels. Her hair was twisted on top of her head in a clip. She'd been instructed to let it loose when the meal was ready, or the moment Avery arrived.

"And he's so delicious," Maggie relished the words. "I may have to press my face to the glass in the breezeway later on." She raised her index finger, "Note to self, bring a towel to wipe off the steam."

Jess laughed. She had only known Maggie for a few months but adored her candor and obvious devotion to Tory. "So catch me up," Jess winked at Maggie. "You met Avery at a rescue?"

"No, shopping," Maggie corrected. "Wait that's not right, they spent the night in the barn."

Tory's eyes narrowed, "Not quite accurate." She turned away from the stove and looked into the expectant faces. "Maggie is, as usual, over romanticizing."

"Not possible," Maggie's laughter floated, "but continue."

Tory shook her head, "Doc Webb offered Avery an internship and..." Her phone alert sounded. Her excitement extinguished, along

143

with the flame beneath the pan. The dress flew up and over her head as she scampered to her bedroom. The soft material landed in a pile in the middle of the bed. She kicked shoes into the closet, released her hair, and intertwined the tresses in record time. Jeans, sweater, and boots were tugged in place. She raced back to the kitchen where Jess and Maggie stood dumbstruck.

Tory scooped up her phone, drafted a fast text to Avery canceling dinner and disappeared from the cottage.

Jess's mouth closed with a snap. "Well."

"I'll say," Maggie bobbed her head in agreement. "The girl can strip clothes like paid professional."

<hr />

The rescue had been one of circumstance, not cruelty. A neighbor reported, out of concern, an elderly rancher who had lost her husband. The woman, overwhelmed by grief, needed aid with relocating her animals. Over tea and sugar cookies, Tory gathered the names of neighbors, and inventoried her livestock. It would be a successful venture all around, and exactly the objective for speaking at the fair.

Tory climbed in her rig. The blue light on her phone flashed. A text message from Avery 'GOOD TIMING AFTER ALL — PICKED UP A CALF, STRAINED MY BACK - SEE YOU TOMORROW IF I'M VERTICAL'.

It wasn't out of her way exactly. Tory angled her truck behind Avery's, and set the parking brake. No dogs to sound her arrival, she stepped on the porch and tested the door. Unlocked, as it should be in the country, she pushed the door open, and walked inside.

"Avery?" She lifted her voice.

"Tory?" His groggy reply met her ears, followed by an agonizing grunt.

"Don't get up," she called. "I'm coming in."

"Don't...I'm..." he cursed. "Wait."

She froze at the door to the living room, and took in the sight of Avery stretched out flat on his back in nothing but his boxers. It would have been awkward, or at least a fraction humorous, if it weren't for the pain marring his face.

"Be still," she moved swiftly and snatched the quilt from the back of the couch. "I'm going to cover you."

His distress softened to an ache of unease, "Not at my best here, Tory."

"I'll fix that," she said easily.

"What are you doing?"

"Shh, close your eyes. I'll be back in a minute."

He heard the bathroom door open, and the sound of water running. He followed her movements back to the kitchen. The microwave hummed then offered a ding of completion.

"Keep your eyes closed, and try to relax." She turned the blanket back, exposed the top of his chest.

"Tory..."

"Hush, I need you to let everything go," she laid a heated moist towel on his collar bone. "Let me help you."

Avery sighed as the heat seeped into stiff muscles.

"Your body has protected itself by holding unnaturally still." Her tone, a muted whisper, drifted over him like her feathered touch. "Now, even more tissue is inflamed and angry." The towel was removed and replaced... Fingers slid and soothed, and a faint fragrance filled the air.

He floated away...aware of nothing but the sensation of Tory's hands eliminating the sharpest edges of his pain. At some point she'd asked him to roll. Vaguely conscious, he obeyed. She lifted his lower legs, placed pillows beneath his shins. His back wept with relief. Heat lessened the tension gripping his spine, while nimble digits kneaded, and calmed. The glide of her palms guided him to cataleptic bliss.

CHAPTER TWENTY-NINE

"Good Morning, Jess," Ginny settled the platter on the bar. "We're going buffet style this morning. The men will be in from the barn shortly, and Tory is in the dining room grumbling about the fair. I made all her favorites but," Ginny tipped her head and mouthed, "tread lightly."

Remi's tail thumped as Jess stepped into the dining room. "Looks like you have a ton of great pictures to choose from." She placed a cup of tea beside Tory's clenched fist.

Tory grunted and shuffled the stacks across the dining room table.

"Doing a before and after? Very smart."

The scented tea swirled and invaded Tory's haze of frustration. She lifted the cup and sipped, then her malleable focus zeroed in on Jess. "Thank you," she drank again, "for the tea, for tidying my kitchen last night, and for hanging up my dress."

"Don't forget those incredible shoes, Maggie was distraught until she located the second one beneath your bed," Jess's eyes sparkled. She raised her cup, "You're welcome."

Tory stared at the images and her scrawled outline highlighting the information she wanted to present at the fair. "People should just do the right thing and give their money." Poncho nudged her elbow, lifting it enough to slide his head onto her lap. "You agree with me, don't you boy?"

"Bummer about your dinner plans."

"It worked out okay in the end," Tory's smile was slow and secret.

Jess's brow winged high. "Maggie tells me pastry unlocks all your secrets. Should I grab you a croissant?"

Tory giggled, "Maybe later."

Riley raced in and nipped a sausage off the platter. "Aren't you hungry, Mom?"

"I'll get something in a bit."

"I can't wait until tonight! Are you excited, Aunt Tory, or has the fair lost the childhood appeal since you are, you know," he grabbed another link, "older?"

"Riley," Jess's reprimand lost effect when it was punctuated with a snicker, "get a plate and sit, barbarian." She cleared her throat and reached for a stern tone, "Apologize to Aunt Tory."

"No harm," Tory waved her off. "It's a good idea actually, thanks Riley. I should try to remember the things I like most about the fair."

Riley loaded his plate, "Do you think it will be like the festival on Chincoteague?"

"I think it will be similar, but without the wild ponies."

"Yeah, and Cora gets to ride for all those people, while Aunt Tory begs. That will be so cool."

Tory whimpered, and laid her head on the wooden table. She deliberately focused on ice cream, funnel cakes, bright lights, and fried everything.

Tory decided to lighten her mood by doting all her attention on Ariel. She passed the hours brushing, bathing, and then lingered over some reflexology, before walking her into the rear pasture and releasing her to run free with three other horses.

Riley raced toward the gate. "Hey champ, slow your feet. You don't want to startle Ariel. She's just settling in."

"Dad said she's healing fast," he frowned. "So now you'll give her away."

It was a harsh reality of tending and owning livestock, but the lesson was important. "First things first, Riley, Ariel isn't mine. I was only put in charge of helping her get strong and healthy."

"You kept Star," he kicked the bale of straw beside the fence.

"I was entrusted with Star, big difference." Tory switched subjects, "Cora's due in a bit."

"Why is she still taking lessons when she owns the horse?"

"There's always something new to learn, but no lesson today. Cora needs to get Star loaded for the fair. She might want your help getting him ready."

"I could help out with that."

She watched Riley jog back to the barn, "Youthful energy," she muttered and climbed atop the gate. A few yards away, Ariel nibbled fresh spring grass.

A truck roared down the lane, drove straight to the back pasture, tossing gravel as it slid to a halt. It took a moment for Tory to align face and name. Ariel's owner. She boosted off the fence and into the pasture, putting the gate between them.

The man slammed out of the vehicle. The punch of whiskey hit Tory a second before his meaty fists grasped the gate.

"May I help you?"

"Visiting my property," he shook the aluminum. "Just because you're feeding her doesn't make her yours."

"She's grazing. Would you like to call her? I'm sure she'll be happy to see you." Ears pinned flat, Ariel snorted and backed away from the fence. Her tail swished violently before she bolted for open pasture. "Perhaps another time," Tory relaxed as she spotted Murphy and Dale rushing from the barn.

"You think you're funny, you smug bitch. Steal them, saddle them, and sell them to rich brats. You'll not take what's mine."

"I follow the law," Tory clipped with calm fury. "And at the moment the law sides with me. I've read the preliminary paperwork on your appeal. Dotting all the I's and crossing every T won't hide the history of your abuse and neglect."

"You and the veterinary saint planted that carcass," rabid eyes spun and he spotted the men closing in. "You'll pay for your lies! You'll not steal what's mine!" He shouted and hurried to his truck.

"You alright?" Dale asked, while Murphy relayed the license information to law enforcement.

"Nothing a hot shower won't fix."

CHAPTER THIRTY

Adorably endearing, Cora and a striking, healthy Star, circled the small riding arena. Tory held the microphone for thirty minutes promoting the goals of the Equine Advocates. She touted education, and addressed the need for monetary help with treatment and fostering of animals who had been victimized. She spoke to the expense law enforcement incurred investigating and pursuing justice. She emphasized the commitment assumed with animal ownership.

"People need to think hard before taking on the responsibility of caring for another life. They also need to feel comfortable reaching out to the authorities before situations become dangerous or inhumane. The Equine Advocates should be a last resort, but when a need arises, their goal is to find and secure safe, permanent placement."

Following the presentation, Cora posed with Star and beamed into any lens aimed her direction. Tory fielded questions and tolerated photos before edging from the limelight. She moved within the shadows of the crowd and climbed into the solitude of her rig. "Going to hide for fifteen precious minutes," she mumbled and eased the seat back, "just fifteen."

The passenger door whipped opened and Avery hopped in beside her.

Butterflies took flight in her belly, "I didn't know you were here."

"Promised Cora I would come to see her. You're a natural. You educated rather than begged. Those people got knowledge for every dollar they stuffed in the jar."

"Better way to look at it," she studied him for any signs of residual discomfort. "Feeling better?"

"Much," his gaze traveled over her face. "I had this really cool dream, or possibly a hallucination…you were in it." Tory opened her mouth to speak. Avery silenced her by pressing a finger against her lips. "It's your turn to hush," he said quietly. His eyes sparked with mischief, his lips quirked in a crooked grin, "Wanna make out?"

———

Tory's palm stroked the empty leather seat, still warm from Avery's body. She should attempt to tamp down the feelings he spurred. The ache inside mocked her. Too late for self-preservation, he had the power to hurt her. When he left she'd have to deal with it.

It was time to load up Star, and return to the ranch. Tory climbed from the rig and paused to enjoy the sight of the fair in full swing. Soon the sun would set, the lights would brighten the midway, and the bandstand would pulse to life. She thought of Riley. No, she wasn't too old to appreciate the festive atmosphere. In fact, she decided she would track down Avery and take a spin on the Ferris wheel.

One second Tory was visualizing the neon, the next she was on the ground. Her hip sang on impact. Infuriated to find herself in the straw, she flipped over.

Ariel's owner was bearing down on her, his fists pounding like King Kong against his chest. Incoherent fury pelted her like hail as he closed the distance.

Tory scrambled backwards like a crab on sand. Her arms instinctively enveloped her head. But instead of the blow to her face, or the brunt of his boot shattering her ribs, she heard a sharp curse followed by a muffled grunt. Tory peeked through her shield and saw the enraged man airborne. In a blink his form was boosted by belt loops and biceps, and hauled away.

Security swarmed the area.

Tory was scrutinized for injuries. "I'm fine," she brushed probing hands away. "He surprised and frightened me, I'm good," she assured the medical tech. Her voice spiked, "Thank you for your concern but I'm fine."

Lauren, president of Equine Advocates pushed through the throng. "Bastard got to you, twice."

"Public place this time," Tory held an ice pack against her hip. "I wish him the best of luck twisting the facts. We've got plenty of witnesses, none of which are related to, or employed by me."

"The magistrate will revoke his appeal for sure."

"I would hope," Tory looked at Lauren, "I'm done for the day, right?"

"You've more than fulfilled your promise. I don't know how to thank you."

"You could remember this incident, and next year, find another volunteer."

Lauren chuckled, "Deal."

Tory gathered up her satchel and limped to her rig. She was going to have a bruise the size of Texas tomorrow.

CHAPTER THIRTY-ONE

"I mean it, Tory," Maggie's voice, fraught with worry, rose above the sound of the rushing water. "That man is a menace."

"No argument," Tory lathered her hair while the spray pounded against her skin. "I expect the regional police will be calling any moment for my formal statement."

"They should take the report in person."

"Uniforms don't have the same effect on me," Tory wrapped the plush towel around her torso. She had showered away the violation, but still felt shaky.

"You're getting multicolored already," Maggie shook her head.

"Trust me, I got off lucky with a bruise. He was scary furious."

"At the wrong person," Maggie left the bathroom, called over her shoulder. "I'm getting you fresh ice."

Tory walked into her bedroom, and scanned the damage in the full length mirror, "Definitely colorful."

"Lucky you had your very own personal, white knight."

"My white what?"

"Avery," Maggie hopped on the bed and pulled her knees under her chin. She giggled at Tory's baffled expression. "You have no idea what I am talking about, do you?"

"I saw him moments before," Tory's cheeks heated. "A little necking in the front seat of the truck."

"Nice. Well lucky for you, after climbing from the love wagon, he didn't get too far. From what I hear Avery was like the Hulk," Maggie fanned her face, "In-cred-ible." She fell back on the pillows, "Minus the shredded clothes and green flesh, of course."

Tory pulled a sweatshirt over her head. Her cell phone rang.

Maggie scooped it up, "Speaking of Mr. Marvel."

"Avery is scarcely a comic strip character."

"You're right. Avery is a flesh and blood real man." She dangled the phone toward Tory, "Lucky you."

Tory tapped the screen, and sent Avery's call to voicemail.

"That wasn't very friendly."

Tory shrugged, she didn't want to add vulnerable crush to her growing list of interactions with Avery. "I have a ton of things to do tonight."

"Me too," Maggie scooted off the bed. "Another penis cake, they could become my specialty." She grabbed her friend's hands. "Are you sure you're alright? We need a little girl time."

"I'm good. I should find Avery, and thank him," she frowned when her text alert chirped.

"Persistent," Maggie hummed.

Tory blew out a breath, "Guess I could invite him to a quiet dinner."

"Dining with your very own determined champion, HOT."

"Maggie," Tory groaned then giggled.

"Sleep-over tomorrow night," Maggie stated rather than asked. "Be safe, have fun, and text me the instant you get home," she whirled from the room.

Tory strolled into the barn and spotted Peach linked in the stable cross ropes. Dale ran a soft brush over her, withers to spine. Across from him, Avery reclined against a stall, boots crossed at the ankle. Dale kicked the dirt and tossed the implement into the grooming tote. He extended his hand toward Avery, and they exchanged a solid shake.

Tory discarded the melted ice pack, and walked toward them.

When he saw her, Avery jammed his hands deeply into his pockets, but not before she caught a glimpse of his scraped and bruised knuckles.

Dale scrutinized Tory, follicles to scarred boots. "Bastard get any licks on you?"

"No," she rubbed her hip. "I just landed hard."

"Good," Dale snapped the lead to Peach's halter. "We're relocating Peach and Titan so the birthing stalls will be available when we need them." He turned to Avery, "I'll be ready for Titan in ten minutes." Dale would've sworn the air sizzled. He cleared his throat, "Umm, well, you take your time."

Avery's attention had drifted far from the colt and the job at hand. He shifted closer to Tory.

She tugged his hand free of his jeans, touched the edges of the abrasion. "I didn't know you were still nearby."

"I stopped to talk to Cora, heard the ruckus. That guy's plenty ticked about you seizing his animals."

"If he'd have cared for them they wouldn't have been taken. His idiocy won't help the next time he's in court. Showing up here, and at the fair," she shook her head slowly, "the fool is nailing his own coffin."

Avery couldn't wait any longer, he had to touch her. He trailed his fingers along the side of her face. His lips brushed her temple, "You're sure you're alright?"

"I'm fine."

When he'd seen her hit the ground, he thought he'd go mad. Unfortunately removing her assailant meant he wasn't able to pick her up and cart her off to safety. "I was frightened, then angry, and then I couldn't find you." His hands trailed the length of her arms.

"It's okay," Tory turned her face into the crook of his neck, "I'm okay, Avery." His tenderness calmed her.

Somewhere deep in the barn a horse whinnied. The moment changed from comfort to combustion in a flash. Avery's arms encompassed her. He lifted, and in two strides ducked them into an empty stall. He feasted on her mouth, giving her no option to refuse the intensity of his assault.

Tory gripped his shoulders. She boosted and wrapped her legs firmly around his hips. She pushed, reckless and ready, against him.

Avery groaned into her mouth as bruising fingers clenched her hips. Tory squeaked as his hands brushed over the sensitive spot on her rump.

"Sorry, sorry," he said in a breathless rush. "You're wounded and I'm treating you…"

"Like I've never been treated before," Tory laid her palms against his cheeks. She released her legs, and settled unsteady feet into the straw. "Sorry, I forgot about your back."

"No complaints," Avery kissed the corner of her mouth, the tip of her nose. "I have a dream therapist."

He eased back, shook his head clear. Tory stood before him, cheeks blushed with passion, chest rising, and falling with her tumble of breath. He heard Peach's maternal nicker. "Momma's calling, I need to get Titan." Avery linked their fingers, drew them into the aisle, and lifted the lead from the hook. "I need to get back to the clinic but, if you're not too tired, you could swing by my place tonight."

"That would be nice." Tory leaned over the stall door, and giggled as Titan danced out of reach.

"If you would stop fighting me," Avery gentled the spirited foal. "You'd see this punishment ends with a reunion with your mother." The lead connected to the metal circle, and the man versus hoof tug of war renewed.

A muttered curse, and a neigh of discontent, brought a fresh smile to Tory's face. Finally the two moved in disjointed unity.

"Not as easy as it looks," Avery grinned. Titan increased his pace carrying him along with the tide.

She laughed, and followed them to the barn door. "See you in a few hours, I'll bring last night's dinner."

"Sounds fantastic."

Chapter Thirty-Two

Avery leaned over the porch railing. He'd heard Tory's rig coming down the lane. He met her in the drive, drew her into the circle of his arms and kissed her lightly. The next kiss offered a punch. Tory's body heated instantly. With effort she broke the connection, "I have a date planned, if you'll indulge me."

"I seem to recall inviting you." Avery attempted to draw her close again, Tory sniggered and twisted away.

She was female enough to allow Avery to help her haul in the tote and cooler from the truck. She carried a canvas bag of linens, and a wicker pie basket inside, and placed them on the counter.

"Wine?"

"Sure," Tory wandered deeper into the apartment. "There was a time I thought I would live here. Doc Webb is my father in many ways." She ran her hands over the back of the vintage red vinyl kitchen chair. "I was a rambunctious teen, pushing boundaries like the best of them. I'd escape to this apartment and spend all afternoon reading."

"Wild and raucous?" Avery chuckled, "with your nose buried in your book."

She cocked her head to the side, "You don't know what I was reading." She unsnapped the tote, and unloaded containers.

"How can I help?"

"Preheat the oven, and give me a bowl for the salad." They worked in tandem to set the small enamel topped table. Tory placed the casserole dish on the top shelf. "Salad now, or with dinner?"

"I can wait."

Tory opened the fridge, noticed the calendar fastened on the door. X's marked off the dates of Avery's time in Montana. "Is this your get-out-of-Dodge countdown?"

"Easy to lose track of time when you're busy," he opened the cupboard and set a large glass bowl on the counter. "I can't believe Webb will be home in two days. Bet he'll be grateful the clinic is still standing."

Tory tapped her finger on another date circled in bright red, "Philadelphia?"

"Marks the end of the intern program. All graduate students convene in Philly to gloat over experiences, and boast about the coveted positions they've landed."

"And this?" She pointed to a starred date.

"My first day of work, in Maryland."

"You said yes."

"Nothing signed yet. I'm flying out Sunday to see the facility, talk terms and contracts. The internship end and the proposed start date in Maryland are only two weeks apart. I want to squeeze in a quality visit with my Mom, and steal a day or two for vacation."

Tory's heart fractured. With effort she smiled, and lifted her wine, "To dreams coming true." The clink of glass veiled the anguish in her voice.

His phone rang, "Talk about timing, it's Maryland. Excuse me one minute."

She turned her back and gathered her riotous emotions. She listened as Avery confirmed details of his trip, a few days from now.

Tory topped off their glasses, as Avery returned to the kitchen. "Vacation where?"

"Nothing planned, it's doubtful I'll be doing anything other than condo hunting, shopping for furniture and a professional wardrobe. Maybe I should have you design my interior, once I find a place."

The thought of building a home for him made Tory miserable. The oven timer sounded, and she busied herself with plating the meal. When she turned Avery was touching a match to a candle in the center of the table. The soft flicker danced over the wall.

Avery lifted his shoulder. "Is this alright?"

"It's perfect."

Tory dried her hands and threaded the tea towel through the oven handle. She moved to the table and extinguished the smoldering candle. In the shadows of the cozy kitchen the dark spiral of smoke swirled. Tory summoned her most confident self before twisting around. Avery stowed the leftovers in the refrigerator. She leaned her hip against the enamel top, "You want dessert?"

Avery snapped to attention. His lips quirked and he crossed the few feet separating them. He lifted his hand and brushed a stray tendril away from her face. "Tell me your plan for the rest of the evening, before I ruin the schedule."

Tory's hands slid to his waist, and pulled his neatly tucked shirt, until it hung loose. "My plan is flexible." Her fingertips boldly trailed the line between denim and flesh. Her hands paused on the silver button of his jeans.

Avery shivered, and clasped her wrists, "No." He leaned in, this time holding her clever fingers away from his body. He took her mouth in a slow tortuous seduction of lips, teeth, tongue. He eased back, "Let's watch a movie."

Tory whined with frustration. She knew he was attempting to hold a line of propriety, just as she knew she was going to make him cross it.

Avery tugged and led her toward the loveseat. Tory folded into the corner, as he cued up *It's Complicated*.

She waited twenty painful minutes before she faced Avery, and initiated a kiss that spoke to frustrations, to longing, and offered more.

"Tory," Avery broke the kiss and shook his head. He didn't know her long enough to be so swamped with clawing need.

She climbed into his lap, laid her palm against his face, and willed him to look at her, to see her, to want her. She kissed him again without providing an opening for interruption. Her hands trailed over his shoulders, down his arms. She brought his hands to her mouth, and touched her lips to each tip.

Her eyes, bright with innocence, and desire, slashed Avery's control. "It's not reasonable to want you the way I do."

Tory drew his hand over her throat, and lower... watched his gaze follow the trail, "Touch me."

His hands gripped her waist, and in a quick move, he set her aside, and surged to his feet. He flicked off the television, the corner lamp, and then walked to her.

Tory placed her hand on his and stood. Avery's hands dropped to her hips, and urged her forward. She closed the distance and pressed fully into him.

Their joint hum of pleasure was smothered when hungry mouths met.

CHAPTER THIRTY-THREE

Tory had a moment to appreciate the vibrant woven wool runner lining the hallway, as Avery dragged her along the narrow hall. She stepped into the master bedroom. The sleigh bed was all function but beyond that, the room was pure fantasy. An alcove, framed with windows, overlooked an endless view of Montana landscape, and the mountains beyond. Mismatched dressers, antique and heirloom, blended with modern practicalities.

Tiny fires licked over her skin, and raced down her spine. The ease and skill of Avery's kiss washed over her. His hands roamed her back, his lips cruised her cheek, and neck. Tory's pulse quaked.

"Your hair," Avery tugged the simple ponytail holder from the end of her braid. "I fantasize about your hair." Tory moaned as he loosened the strands and massaged her scalp.

"Avery…" she breathed. When her hair hung loose, he went to work on the tiny buttons of her shirt. "Too many," he complained, "trying to torture me?"

"Not on purpose," The air hit her skin. She instinctively pulled the fabric closed. Modesty, he smiled, and lifted her chin with his finger. He brushed her hair aside, exposing the line of her neck. He placed his lips against her thundering pulse.

His tenderness muddled her mind. A hum purred in her throat and erupted in a shivering moan of pleasure. Tory's mind shut off, she relaxed fully and framed Avery's face with her hands. "Your eyes did it for me. You have a fierce concentration like you're waging war with what you want, and what you think is best."

"You confound me."

She pressed her lips to his cheek, whispered, "I don't mind being a puzzle, but I want you to listen to what I'm telling you." She kissed him deeply, taking until he was as breathless as she. "Whatever seduction, or romance, you think I need, toss it aside. A long time ago I set my standard and waited…for you. It's been a long wait, and I'm tired of being patient. So hear me, Avery, I don't want flowers, music, fancy food… I only want you."

He lifted her, fell onto the bed, covered her, and plundered.

Tory's breath caught, hitched, sobbed as Avery drove her toward some unseen summit.

"Relax," he whispered.

"Impossible," she released a tense laugh.

Avery levered up on his elbows and for his own pleasure fanned out the heavy seduction of her hair.

Her hair, Tory smiled. Men were fascinated by the oddest things.

Avery kissed her, wistful, and dreamy. The weight of his body spiked the anticipation. He had never found himself in a situation that evoked such hunger. Avery rolled, and pulled her with him. Their fingers laced and tugged until torsos aligned. Clothing fell away, and each inch of exposed flesh was savored.

Sensation spiraled to another level of longing Tory hadn't known existed. Desire amplified until it exploded. She whimpered against his lips… "Show me."

Tory lay tangled in the comforter. Sated, she guessed was the word, or perhaps she had arrived underdressed in the afterlife. The mattress shifted beneath her. The bathroom door opened, then clicked closed, and she lacked the energy to raise her eyelids.

Unsteady on his feet, Avery braced his hands on the bathroom counter. He breathed deeply and hoped the Earth would settle on its axis. Tory Keen…he was in a heap of trouble. He looked in the mirror, and didn't recognize the man staring back at him. He cupped his hands beneath the stream of water, and doused his face.

"Avery?" Tory's voice carried faintly through the door. "If you happen to have a cup in there I'd kill for a sip of water."

He pinched his eyes tight in a last ditch effort to gather himself. We're rational adults, consenting, logical, somewhat lucid, no hearts involved, grownups. He ran the tap on cold, filled the glass, and returned to the bedroom.

Moonlight pushed through the paned glass like a spotlight on the leading lady. Her hair was tousled over the pillow. The disheveled bedding hugged her curves like an erotic pinup.

She smiled like a lazy cat, and rolled to her side. The comforter dipped lower exposing additional enticing angles. Avery's insides bunched. "I don't think my knees have ever gone weak at the sight of a woman before."

Tory sat up and raked her hands through her tangled hair. "Thanks," she took the glass and sipped.

Avery sat gently on the mattress, "I want to hear about Kentucky, but I keep getting sidetracked."

She tucked a hunk of wild hair behind her ear, "At this point recounting the events is more energy than I want to give. Let's just say dream opportunities can look very different when they're served on a platinum platter."

"Disappointed?"

"Not as much as you'd expect. My goal ultimately, was positive exposure for equine massage therapy. We'll get that. I just wasn't the right fit in a therapist, or more apt, they weren't the right avenue for me. I'm good with it."

Avery pushed to his feet, and stepped away from the bed.

Tory willed him to say something more, to fill the silence of the room. Instead he struck a match, and ignited the oil lamp on the dresser. The flickering light danced across the walls and ceiling. Tory's mouth dried all over again when Avery's gaze landed on her. Ravenous eyes traveled the length of her body.

"Need more water?" She shook her head. "Good."

Chapter Thirty-Four

Tory hurried into the barn before dawn, grateful Dale's truck wasn't parked out front. Tension released from her shoulders. She'd cleared the first hurdle of the morning. Everyone would simply assume she'd just begun her day extra early.

She hustled to the tack room to grab a work coat, turned the corner, and smashed straight into Murphy.

"Good morning," he circled the polishing cloth over the saddle balanced on his knee. "Getting an early start?"

"Apparently, not early enough," she muttered and snagged a jacket. "I'm going to saddle Ariel, and see how she handles a rider." Tory could feel her brother's eyes on her. A pink flush tinted her neck and cheeks. She didn't want to be scolded, or teased.

"Tory," Murphy stopped his busy hands, "he's leaving."

She wanted to be angry, but the sadness in Murphy's tone had her looking up. Instead of fire, she sighed and laid her hand on his shoulder, "When he does, I'll survive it."

Murphy gripped her fingers. The squeeze transferred all his unspoken concerns.

"Doc Webb is home today," he commented.

"I expect he'll bring the goats midday." Her phone vibrated, "It's Maggie. She's going to want every detail about..." Tory cast her eyes to the floor, "about the fair." She clicked the line, and hurried out of the stable. "Hey."

"You, my friend, are a party in a box." Maggie's laugh was like wild beams of light chasing dawn, "Where shall we begin?"

"How much coffee have you had?"

"Who counts? Besides it's your fault. I got sleepy... One cup, two cups, three, gotta stay awake... my friend is calling after her hot, hero, yum-yum fest. Pod in, pod out, pod in, just push a button… Flavored or plain, caffeine or not, tea, cocoa, chai, and cider… Did you know they have cider? Can't possibly be real apples, poor unfortunate apples, turned to powder and stuffed into a recyclable container."

"For the love of all things holy," Tory released a bemused lungful of air. "If I were still tucked in bed I'd hang up on you."

"You're up and out? I hoped to catch you before you hit the barn. Planned on leaving a contemptuous message, but in person chatting is so much better. Don't you think?"

"I don't know, you're doing all the talking, and I certainly don't want to be yelled at before the sun has formally risen."

"I'm coming over."

"Maggie?" Silence met Tory's ears. She lowered the device and stared at the screen. "She hung up on me."

Tory circled Ariel on the lunge line. The mare handled the saddle like a dressage champion.

"She's looking great." Maggie waved a thirty-two-ounce bottle of water. "Flushing caffeine from my system or at the very least, diluting the potency." Her eyes narrowed to considering slits, "Hmmm…"

"What?"

"Not a thing," she sang. "From your smile, and lack of phone call, one could presume?"

"Your imagination needs little encouragement."

"Aww," Maggie swooned. "That's so sweet and I'll admit, I'm a wee bit jealous."

"Don't be, this particular bolt of sunshine comes with an aggressive dimmer switch." Tory reeled Ariel in and walked toward the rail. "Avery's internship is ending."

Maggie hooked her elbow over the fence, "He won't go."

"Of course he will," Tory snapped. Ariel snorted, and hopped to the side. "Easy girl," Tory took a measured breath, and forced herself to relax. "How'd your cake turn out?"

"Great. You're coming over later to eat it. Bring Jess. I'll tell you about the stroke of caffeine inspired brilliance I had at three in the morning."

―――

Avery woke and knew his bed and home were empty. The quick pang in his chest chastised him. He should have taken more care. He rolled to his back and groaned.

A text alert sounded. Avery bounded across the room. Enthusiasm took a nose-dive, when he saw it was just the morning update from the clinic. He sat heavily on the disheveled bed, cradled his head in his hands. Cell rang again, he lunged toward the dresser. This time disappointment was wrapped in the lifeline he desired. He slid his thumb across the screen, "Hi Mom."

"Seventy-two hours and we'll share the same time zone," delight peppered her words.

"Time went fast."

"What's wrong?"

"Nothing, Doc Webb comes back tomorrow and I have a lot to finish before I can focus on the next phase."

"Just take one day at a time, and look forward to the break between the two. I hope you're planning to stay with me for a few days. I'd like to have you beneath my roof so I can spoil you, before you settle in Maryland."

"That's my plan," Avery wandered to the dresser and pulled out clothes for the day. "I'm heading to the clinic now."

"It's early."

"Veterinarian's schedule in Montana hardly resembles banker's hours." He chuckled, "I've slept with a pager for two weeks."

"Now you sound like an emergency room nurse," she laughed lightly. "I can tell you're in a hurry. Call me when you have time to talk, and if you see your friend Maggie, tell her thank you in advance, for the recipes."

CHAPTER THIRTY-FIVE

From his truck Avery watched Tory stack split logs beside her cottage.

She'd fled his home before daybreak without sentiment, or drama. She'd driven home and jumped into her day, business as usual.

He should be elated and leaping over the distant mountains, but instead found the casual move irritated him.

He sat captivated as she pulled off her coat and hat in an erotic lumberjack strip tease. She centered a solid block of wood onto the chopping stump, then hefted the heavy blade. The ax plunged into the flesh of the log. With a deft jerk she freed the weapon to circle again. Tory's braided tail punctuated each precise blow of steel, until the log splintered, and separated into two chunks.

Avery scrubbed his hands over his weary face. There was something between them, and he needed to figure out what it was before he headed home. Fascinated to the point of annoyance, Avery climbed from the truck.

Tory tensed when she spotted Avery. "Hey," she set the ax aside and crouched to load her arms with wood.

Avery reached down and gathered the remaining pieces off the ground, "May I come in?"

Tory nudged the door to her cottage with her hip, "I'm not heating the outside."

He stepped to her cast iron wood rack, dropped the logs in place, then snagged the broom, and gathered the fallen splinters. "You left early."

His voice tickled over her skin, sparking memories of the murmurs they'd shared only hours ago. "Figured it was best, I had things to take care of this morning," Tory stripped her gloves, and crouched to tend the fire. "I still have a lot to..."

"I'm familiar with this particular dance," Avery interrupted.

"Huh?"

"You, dismissing me," he scooped the mess into a dust pan, walked to the door and tossed the dirt outside. "I call it the Tory two-step."

Tory stood, and propped her hands on her hips, "You're angry."

He stared at her puzzled expression, "I'm not angry."

"I may not have experience with the 'morning after' but I can tell you're annoyed about something."

He paced to the kitchen counter, pressed his palms on the flat surface, and blew out a breath. "I'm annoyed that you preferred performing laborious tasks instead of waking with me, and lingering over breakfast."

She flushed, "Oh."

"I'd like to take you to dinner tonight. Webb is home tomorrow and between the clinic reports and..."

"You don't need to take me to dinner," Tory interrupted. "Besides I have plans." She skirted the island, reached for the refrigerator, "Juice?" She squeaked when Avery snagged her shirt, and dragged her tight against him.

The hug, rigid and rough, spoke to his exasperation. He gentled his hands and looked down into wide eyes. "Perhaps I am angry, but not with you." His mouth lowered and his lips were gentle and sweet. "Time and circumstance have given me a short stick." The next kiss was deep and possessive. His lips left hers to hum over her throbbing pulse. "Waking to discover you gone was an unwelcome kick," he poured every ounce of emotion into the next scorching kiss.

Tory clung, her breath shuddered. "I could do an early dinner, but it's girls' night. I'll just pack an overnight bag, and you can drop me at Maggie's."

"I had other plans," his brow wrinkled, "and certainly a better use for your overnight bag."

"I think it's for the best all around. You have paperwork and I have..." to figure out how to continue to exist after your departure. "We don't want the milk to spoil, or the fruit to rot."

"What?"

"Nothing," Tory leaned in, and savored his mouth on hers. She forced the corners of her mouth into a cheerful smile, "Dinner will be nice. What time should I be ready?"

CHAPTER THIRTY-SIX

Avery had hoped to take Tory somewhere fancy and deserving of her dress and heels. Unfortunately since she had evening plans with the girls, they had to stick close to home. He drove them to the brew pub near the college.

Crowded and noisy, the bar was a bustle of bodies. There was a game on, and apparently the favored team was playing well. Another setback in sticking to Tory's hometown turf was she knew everyone.

The small talk and casual exchanges were killing him. Each intrusion stole precious minutes of his limited time with Tory. "I should have made dinner for you at my place."

"You don't like the pub?"

"I don't care for the crowd," he muttered as another person walked over. Tory laughed at something the woman said. Her face, lit with genuine contentment, dimmed as her eyes flicked back to Avery's. She placed her hand over the woman's, and joked about ignoring her date.

"I'm sorry, I never run into people, well correction, I rarely come out. It seems as if everyone is here tonight." She lifted her shoulder in apology. "Small town perk, or curse, I'm not sure."

Avery leaned across the small table, "After Webb gets back I only have a few days until…" the waitress reached past him, and cleared their plates.

"You're headed to Maryland, then Philadelphia, exciting times for you," Tory said brightly, while below the table her fingers fisted in her lap. "You'll be living from your suitcase in a fast city, and enjoying total anonymity in any bar of your choosing." She felt her stomach roll and clench with false cheer.

"I'd like you to come to Philadelphia with me."

A roar went up at the bar, muffling Tory's surprised gasp.

"The ceremony would only be one night," Avery continued, "Semi-formal, you can wear a pair of your killer heels. We'd have the whole weekend to see the city. You could meet my mom."

"I doubt I can get away."

Avery hadn't pictured Tory's response to his invitation in any other syllable besides yes. He paid the bill, rested his hand against the small of her back, and guided her to the exit.

How could such simple contact weaken her? It was the forty-seventh thing she'd found endearing since Avery had picked her up. Her dinner tumbled in her gut. His hand on her knee as they drove to dinner, the way he'd offered her a warm roll while frowning at an interruption to their meal.

Tory's conscious sneered and kicked her hard in the shin, as they crossed the parking lot to the truck.

She'd allowed herself to become undermined by impossibility. In less than two weeks, she'd become a fanciful female. This afternoon she'd accused Avery of being angry, now Tory was the one boiling.

He'd invited her to Philadelphia. Like she could drop everything and jump on a plane to the City of Brotherly Love. What did he want from her? Rousing applause as he surged forward into the life he'd dreamed of without her?

She dropped his hand and opened the door, and slid inside without a word. Avery rounded the hood, and climbed in beside her. He glanced over. She was pale, her hands clenched, her knuckles white in her lap. He turned the engine over, and drove to Maggie's.

Tory hopped from the cab the moment the truck stopped. The interior light flashed as the passenger door opened. She would have escaped if Avery hadn't been so quick. He caught her hand, and rotated her body until she faced him.

"I have no idea what magazine article advice is playing in that brain of yours. I invited you to Philadelphia because what's happening between us is important." His eyes pleaded with her, "You don't need to meet my mom, but I'd like you to."

"I appreciate the offer. It would be nice to see the city," her smile failed to achieve authentic. "I'll check with Murphy and Dale, and let you know."

———

Jess watched the exchange from inside the house, "Something's brewing."

"Shove over," Maggie hurried to the window in time to observe Avery's polite kiss. "Ouch, we're going to need to stick our noses in, but be stealthy about it." In a blur, Maggie flew to the kitchen and snagged items from the recesses of her cupboards. "Take her to the living room, all casual, girls being girls. I'll be there in a jiffy."

"Right," Jess turned away from the window, then gestured in confusion. "Do what?"

Maggie snapped her fingers, and pointed, "Living room, be quick. I'll be along in a few minutes with the best crowbar into the female psyche. Calories."

Tory opened the door, and channeled cheerful, "Hi everyone."

"In the living room," Jess called. "Perfect timing, Maggie and I were just deciding on a movie. Wow, I love your dress."

Tory stopped midstride, "I'm sorry, guys." She squeezed her tired and burning eyes tight, and willed the heaviness to release from her chest. "I'm really not up for girls' night. I think I should probably go home."

"Sit a moment, you're upset." Jess lifted the overnight bag from Tory's limp grip and set it on the floor. "You want to change?"

"Not yet," Tory allowed Jess to lead her to the couch. She slipped out of her shoes, folded herself into the corner, draped the chenille spread over her legs, and snuggled deeper into the cushions.

Maggie strolled into the room with three bowls of ice cream balanced on one arm, and a tray of sundae toppings in the other.

"Maggie, I just ate."

"Nobody eats on dates," Maggie fixed Tory's bowl the way she liked it best. "I'm sorry you're unhappy. Let's eat frozen milk and sugar and we'll talk it through."

"Really, don't think I can."

"Talk, or eat?"

Jess snickered.

"Talk first," Maggie laid her palm on Tory's leg. "The cream will be just as tasty when it turns to soup."

"I thought we were eating cake."

"Despite being delectably scrumptious, cake is not the best prescription for what's ailing you. Cake is great for breakfast, ice cream on the other hand, not so much."

"Avery's session with Doc Webb is over and his contract with the practice in Maryland starts in a few weeks." Tory added an additional caloric insult with a heavy dollop of whipped cream. "He was leaving all along. An internship is not a life oath."

The sugar worked to lessen Tory's devastation. She balanced the sundae on her lap and unburdened her heart. Jess and Maggie were great listeners. They were the perfect combination of fortitude, and comfort.

"He asked me to meet him in Philadelphia."

"Romantic," Maggie sighed.

"I'm not going."

"Why not?"

"We had a nice time getting to know each other, and the time is over. I'm not running across the country prolonging the inevitable. I have responsibilities, obligations, and people who count on me."

"And if you didn't?" Jess asked.

"Silly to indulge in fiction, the basic truth is I do." Tory spooned up softened cream and fudge, absorbed the punch of sweetness. "I knew it would end, I'm just sorry it has to, enough about me," Tory waved her hands. "Maggie you promised to share your caffeine induced stroke of genius."

"Ooo, yes," Maggie settled her bowl on the table, and rose to her knees. "I'm going to revolutionize the world of erotic baking," her face lit with excitement. "I have a mock-up for an internet advertisement...somewhere," she gestured broadly, and giggled as she continued. "My brilliant idea, thanks to Tory's oversight in forgetting to call me after her hot date..." Maggie pounded her legs, simulating a drum roll, "Diversity – size, shape, and the entire palette of skin tones. I mean really, if a doctor can ask me to check a box on an insurance form, and a credit card company can require disclosure of my heritage, who am I to discriminate? Globally friendly, that's me."

Jess sat in wide-eyed silence, even as Tory cackled and fell across the couch cushions. The eruption of laughter filled the house. The girls squeaked and wheezed, as they attempted to catch their breath.

Maggie's announcement was a side dish of jubilance to counter Tory's main course of heartbreak. Jess winked at Maggie, lifted her spoon in cheers, and mouthed, "Well done."

CHAPTER THIRTY-SEVEN

Doc Webb met Avery in the driveway, "Pretty convenient having you bunk on my property."

"Welcome home."

"Thanks," they walked toward the truck. "Sounds like you've had a few interesting adventures while I battled the absorption of ultraviolet rays."

"Definitely packed the resume."

"Fantastic," Webb turned the engine over, and patted his pocket in search of his Wrigley's. He offered Avery a stick, then popped a piece into his mouth.

Avery smiled as Webb folded the wrapper into tiny triangles and laid the foil in the cup holder. "What do you do with all your wrappers?

"I don't do anything with them." Webb shook his head, "The wife however, she's clever." His baffled laugh rumbled, "Won't try to explain it. When you're head over tail for the same woman as many years as me, you'll learn some things defy reason and just are."

"Women," Avery said with full male sentiment.

"True," Webb put the truck in gear and cast a sidelong gaze at Avery. "Now that I have you cornered like a parent prepared to lay-out the birds and the bees," his brows wiggled. "It's my turn to give you something to chew on before you fly across the nation. I understand you've had your sights set on Maryland for awhile now, but I'd like to point out the plus side of my little corner of the world."

Avery listened to Doc Webb's persuasive proposal. He was admittedly intrigued by the variety of activities handled by the clinic, and the range of needs throughout the county. He had a lot to consider.

Avery's phone rang as he climbed from the cab. He frowned at the screen, and sent the call to voicemail.

"Problem?"

"No…" Avery braced his hands on his hips, "the Maryland practice is trying to reach me. I'll be on their turf in two days, not sure why they're calling."

"Take a minute, return their call. I'll load the goats."

Tory stood at the railing as Doc Webb carried the smaller goat into the pen. They barely resembled the animals Tory had seen the night of the rescue. Their eyes were brilliant and cheerful, their coats clean and glossy. They were timid but relaxed as they lay on the soft straw.

Her eyes skimmed over the loss of extremities. "I thought you were doing robo limbs."

"They need to heal a bit longer."

"They will not be returned to that bastard's farm."

"No, they won't." Webb lifted the latch and exited the enclosure. He bumped his hip to hers, and offered a stick of gum.

Tory bumped back, folded the paper, and tucked it into her pocket, "Nice tan."

"Something to be said about sunshine, you should try it."

Tory snorted, "So everyone keeps telling me."

"Wife wants to do a fancy dinner reception, after the fact. We renewed our vows on the trip, and purchased a time-share in St. Martin."

"Have mercy, were you drunk?"

"Most of the time, yes," he grinned.

Tory's cell phone chirped. She glanced at the screen, Avery again. It was the third text in an hour.

"Here she goes," Doc Webb inclined his head toward the small goat with double front amputation at the knee. "Have you seen Adrian's party trick?"

"Adrian?"

"To her boy Rocky," Webb grinned. "Love, resilient love." On cue the goat in the straw gathered, and rose from her inclined position until she was standing tall on her hind legs.

"Are you kidding?" Tory shook her head in pure amazement, and moved into the pen.

"She started standing last night, probably sick of craning her neck."

"Aren't you a special one?" The goat teetered toward Tory, and tilted into open arms. Eyes dazzling with emotion, Tory stroked Adrian chest to flank. She grinned at Doc Webb, "You approve of a little acupressure?"

"It's your specialty. Anything you suggest, I approve of."

Tory pressed her face into Adrian's neck. She had known the choice she'd made in Kentucky was right, but now understood, beyond doubt, she'd made the right decision.

Chapter Thirty-Eight

Avery changed clothes and time zones in less than four hours. In Baltimore he had been met at the gate by a chauffeur who handed him a binder with his itinerary for the next two days. He rode in style to the orthopedic practice, enjoyed a catered brunch, and a tour of the sprawling facility. He'd assisted with two surgeries then he was whisked off for a round of golf. The late afternoon indulgences continued over a sixteen-ounce seared steak, and a hundred dollar bottle of wine at the owner's private club.

The sun was setting over the Inner Harbor, as the driver pulled in front of the hotel. Keyed up and drained at the same time, Avery was grateful to have the night to himself.

He entered the suite of rooms, suitable for a family of five. On the sofa table a basket of fruit, and a six-pack of his favorite beer waited. The hand written card thanked him for his flexibility in making the trip a day early. In the master bedroom his bags waited along with a box of chocolates, and a view overlooking the water.

Avery kicked off his shoes, and strolled to the immense glass window. He could see the Ravens' football stadium, the National Aquarium, a landscape speckled with the bustle of commerce.

A far cry from the tranquil mountains of Montana. He leaned his forehead against the glass. She hadn't returned a single call or text. Why he'd expected differently was his problem. It would be easier than ever for Tory to dismiss him with a dozen states between them.

Avery unzipped his luggage and began to fill the bag for the laundry service. His phone vibrated. A glance at the screen and the tension grasping his shoulders loosened, "Hi Mom."

"Quite a whirlwind, how'd your day go?"

Avery lowered to the edge of the bed, "The facility is flawless, state of the art. The staff is impressive. It's everything I expected, and more."

"Then why do you sound unhappy?"

"When I crawled out of bed this morning I hadn't counted on fleeing the Midwest with an hour's notice. I had to ask the concierge to send someone for my laundry."

"Taught you better than to travel with dirty drawers," she chastised. "Was there a valid reason to escalate your travel plans?"

"Complicated surgeries," he sighed. "They wanted an opportunity to show me firsthand the advanced technology waiting in the position."

"Nice to have two prestigious practices fighting over you."

"Webb would love to hear you toss him equally into the mix," he laughed quietly. "I'm a bit overwhelmed to tell you the truth. I could use a little family grounding."

"Really?" Delight brightened her voice. "Is there enough room for me in the hotel they're plying you with?"

Avery chuckled, "It's obscene. The bathtub is big enough for six." A sharp knock sounded on his door, "Hang on, Mom." He snagged the duffle, and walked through the sitting area. "I can't ask you to drive three hours to turn around again."

"Be serious," she clucked her tongue. "You know I love an excuse to exercise my cute SUV. Answer your door."

Avery fished a five from his wallet and pulled the door wide. "Thanks for the prompt...Mom?"

"Hopped in the car as soon as I got your message," she breezed into the room. "The nice lady in personnel provided your hotel information. Good thing I sent those baskets of baked goods," she tossed her bag on the floor. "You weren't kidding. Wow." She faced him with a brilliant smile. "Close the door, Honey, and grab your shoes. We're going to find us a dive bar with live music. Family grounding at your service."

Avery wrapped his arms tight around her, and breathed away the final degree of tension. "You're the best."

CHAPTER THIRTY-NINE

"Hey, Miss Tory," Mike, one of the high-schoolers, hooked his muscled bicep loosely over her shoulder. "Wanna be my date to the prom?"

Tory snickered and looked up into his striking adolescent face. Mike had joined her Friday class as an awkward, acne ridden boy. He'd been a full foot shorter then with braces bracketing his teeth. "I'm not going to a high school dance, even to chaperone."

"Rejected," the unruly cluster jibed in relentless harmony.

Tory ignored her vibrating phone as the energy of youth piled into trucks and cars. She waved until the final taillight vanished from view, then strolled to the barn feeling lighter than she had all day. The dogs trotted at her side. "I got asked to the prom," she petted Remi's head. "What do you think about that?"

Doc Webb and Dale stood in the center of the stable. Tory was about to call out when she caught the tail of their discussion.

"Surprised to see you covering the night shift," Dale lowered to a bale of straw, stretched his legs, and crossed his boots at the ankle. "Why aren't you milking the kid for his final days?"

"Avery asked me to release him this morning. The fancy practice in Maryland wanted to puff their feathers, and strut a few days early. He flew back East before lunch."

"What are they offering?"

Doc Webb shrugged, "A different life."

"Thought he was your guy? Guess you worked him too hard."

"If a veterinarian plans to work any way other than hard, he's in the wrong profession. Can't blame the kid, it's the position he's always wanted. I just hoped he'd want this more."

Dale scrubbed his hand over his face. "Is he coming back?"

"Doubtful," Doc Webb shook his head. "I pitched my offer so he has choices. Hard to outweigh love and loyalty when a mother's tipping the scale."

"Funny, after ducking cupid's arrows for the past week, I assumed Avery had more invested here than veterinary work."

Doc Webb lifted his brows. "Care to fill me in?"

"I'm not much for gossip, but gossip is distorting facts and adding speculation right?"

"I suppose."

"Then I'll tell you straight, your girl fell hard."

Tory's heart squeezed painfully in her chest. Avery was gone. He wasn't coming back. Tears gathered. She glanced over her shoulder. The last thing she needed was Dale and Doc Webb seeing her sniffling.

Her hand flew to her hip. The voice messages she had refused to listen to, the texts she'd refused to open. She eased out the back of the barn and queued up her mailbox. Avery's voice filled her ear.

'YOU MUST STILL BE IN A LESSON. CALL ME WHEN YOU GET THIS. THE MARYLAND PRACTICE SUMMONED, I'M FLYING TO BALTIMORE TODAY, RIGHT NOW. PLEASE COME TO PHILADELPHIA NEXT WEEKEND. I KNOW YOU'RE BUSY BUT... PLEASE COME.'

A sob hitched in her throat. Tory covered her mouth, circled the barn and hopped on the ATV they used to check the fences. The anguish in the pit of her stomach gathered and bloomed. The engine fired, and drowned the sound of her suffering.

She'd tried so hard to remain indifferent and treat her feelings for Avery like a trivial affair she'd watched so many times on the Hallmark channel. Cut to commercial she wanted to scream. Tears scalded her cheeks. She raced through the meadow to the farthest strip of Keen owned property. Beside a spring-swollen mountain stream she shut down the engine. Finally alone with her breaking heart, she allowed the emotion to roll through her.

CHAPTER FORTY

Jess settled into the rocking chair, tossed the quilt across her legs. She and Maggie had agreed Tory should be allowed two days to process Avery's absence.

"A respectful forty-eight hours," Maggie had said. Jess willed Tory to reach out and accept the comfort of her friends, but she hadn't. So under direct orders from Maggie she was staked out in Tory's breezeway, set to interfere.

Poncho whimpered a soft bark, "Hush now." Jess rubbed her hand over the dog and opened a book. "Meddling props," she explained when Poncho tipped his head to the side. "Now lie down and start snoring like we've been here for hours."

Tory delayed leaving the barn until she was certain Ginny had gone home for the evening. Murphy and Jess had taken Riley to town to see a movie. She was grateful to have the house to herself, and even more for her own space. She didn't feel like talking to anyone.

Too late for dinner, too early for bed, Tory stopped in the main kitchen, and poured herself a glass of tea. The mantle clock announced the hour, and the comfort of the quiet enveloped her. She unscrewed the metal lid on the glass jar, and selected a cookie she wasn't hungry for. She'd make a fire and finish her book. She walked into her glass house, and pulled up short at the sight of Jess.

"I'm here to kidnap you," Jess offered an apologetic smile. "We are to report to Maggie's to eat salsa."

"Liar," Tory bit a defiant chunk out of her cookie. "You're supposed to be at the theater with your men, and Maggie rarely serves salsa."

"Strawberry pie is not salsa," Tory scooped a heaping spoonful of dessert.

"The salsa isn't ready yet," Maggie stood over a pot of simmering fragrance and circled the spoon. "Any news from Avery?"

"He left a few messages," Tory pushed away from the table. "Jess? You need a drink?"

"Just water, thanks."

"Water's no good with pie," Maggie tapped her spoon on the side of the pot. "Do we want hot or cold? I'm feeling like an iced mocha."

"Whatever you choose," Tory returned to her chair. "No alcohol, I need to get back to my paperwork."

Maggie bustled, blended, and added flavorings. She placed three glass mugs filled with frozen coffee, and inches of whipped cream sprinkled with shaved dark chocolate, in front of her friends.

"Maggie," Jess moaned. "These look like dessert all by themselves."

"Thanks," Maggie sipped, and focused in on Tory. "Did we reply to Avery's messages?"

"No," Tory raised her cup and licked the cream, "*we* did not reply." She squirmed under the weight of her friends' poignant stares. "What would you have me say?"

"The man invited you to Philadelphia," Maggie returned to the stove.

"I have no time to play tourist. You both are being ridiculous."

Maggie wiped her hands on her apron, "You want ridiculous?" She lifted her laptop, carried it to the table, and tapped a few keys. "Browse the profiles of my computer suitors. I made you a montage." She rotated the screen toward Tory and Jess, "A slide show of pictures for giggles, however it's not amusing, it's pitiable. A bunch of men with backward baseball caps, and tush exposing low-rise jeans, some of whom don't speak English, or live with their parents while they," she framed air quotes and rolled her expressive eyes, "bump up their resumes." The screen filled with a jovial face, minus a front tooth, and a scraggly beard. Another proposed match sported a camouflage beanie and gripped a crushed can of Budweiser.

"Oh Maggie," Jess muffled a snort.

"Then at the polar opposite end of the spectrum, we have Mr. I own a yacht and property in the Caribbean. Over whitened teeth, and Botox injected foreheads…past-their-prime losers, paired with me!" Maggie stood, wiggled her butt, and turned in a slow circle, "Hellloooo, I'm a catch."

"Precisely why I encourage you to stick with real men."

"Exactly," Maggie pointed at Tory. "Go to Philadelphia."

"What does online dating have to do with a man who passed through town on his way to something better?"

"You're an idiot," Maggie eyes filled. "You love him, and if you'd open your eyes you'd see Avery loves you too."

"Maggie, don't cry," Tory withered at the show of compassion.

"We Googled his mom's B&B in Philadelphia," Jess offered. "It looks beautiful."

"I am not calling his mother," Tory snapped.

"You don't have to, we did." Maggie bustled to the stove and stirred her salsa. "Her place is lovely, by the way."

"You what?"

"She's expecting you whenever," Maggie rolled on. "I'm packing a few jars of salsa to give her as a thank you, plus I jotted down a few pastry recipes."

"Maggie…" Tory was weary beyond words. "I'm not going to fly to Philadelphia, and visit with Avery's mother."

"Bethany."

"What?"

"Her name is Bethany Rush," Maggie tapped a few keys on the laptop. "There, look at her Bed and Breakfast, lovely. I refuse to email my secrets but I trust you'll guard them with your life, until you pass them off in person.

Tory folded her arms on the counter, and lowered her head. "Jess, are you planning to help me out, or just sit there while she bulldozes me?"

"I think she's right," Jess's tone was apologetic. "What time's her flight?"

"Whose flight? To where?" Tory absorbed the wave of dread.

"Yours," Maggie shook her head, "to Philadelphia. Honestly Tory, do try to keep up."

CHAPTER FORTY-ONE

Avery's starched shirt felt like briars against his flesh, his tie a noose around his throat. He sipped the cocktail and wished for a cold beer. His companions droned on about fellowships with premier practices, and keys to VIP suites.

"That's not the way to seal the deal," Brice Kenzington raised his voice above the chatter. "You insist on the corner office, a Ferrari, and an assistant with surgically enhanced breasts, and legs to her ears." Brice grinned showing every porcelain veneer. "They called me back in three hours, and asked me what make and model," he paused on an arrogant puff then added, "I told 'em I prefer twenty-three-year-old blondes, but any dazzling dame would do."

Avery turned his back on the peacock. He'd endured Brice through two years of grad school. His diploma freed him from tolerating any more arrogant antics.

A waiter passed with another tray of shrimp puffs reminding Avery his evening had only begun.

Tory stared at the busy city. Those women, her so-called-friends, had ambushed her.

"Oh my gracious." The cab pulled into the hotel carport. A porter opened her door, and another lifted her luggage from the trunk.

"Welcome, Madame, to the Jefferson Regent. Shall I escort you to the front desk, or are you already checked in?"

"I...ah...I have my room already." Well she assumed she did. Tory dug into her jeans and pulled out a few bills for a tip, "Thank you."

What if Avery had changed his mind? He certainly wasn't expecting her to stroll in the front door. What if he was sharing a room? With a woman even. Anxiety threatened to paralyze her limbs.

She left her luggage with the concierge and boarded an elevator. Red numbers counted the floors on the way to the hotel's conference room. The doors slid apart. Laughter and loud music filled the corridor. People spilled from rooms into the halls. Bodies were grouped in clusters much like a college dormitory.

Tory weaved through the throngs of people and muttered, "Frat party minus the college campus." Maybe she had the wrong hotel, certainly the wrong floor, or perhaps she was in the wrong city altogether.

Regardless, Tory knew she'd definitely made a huge mistake.

She followed the hall searching for the stairwell. The corridor widened and became a gallery alcove which opened into a breathtaking ballroom. Crystal chandeliers glinted overhead, and soft music skimmed through the air in light accompaniment to the conversation. Servers circled the space, balancing trays of drinks and mouth-watering tidbits. The room was lined with easels displaying images of the graduates celebrating their accreditation and certification. Tory followed the parade of faces until she was standing in front of a three-by-five foot glossy representation of Avery.

Abruptly conscious of her jeans and boots, Tory tugged the neckline of her shirt. She hadn't given a thought to the dress code for the events of the conference. She only wanted to find Avery. Nerves bounded in her gut like a thousand jack rabbits.

She decided to return to the lobby and regroup. Laughter drew her attention to a group of men by the bar.

Awareness pulled her eye to the man who stood a step apart from the mass. His crisp shirt and tie were a step up from his typical tattered hoodie. She had wanted to find Avery, and here he was.

A boisterous voice carried above the din.

"Avery, I see you survived the wild, wild west." Brice clasped his manicured fingers on Avery's shoulder. "Montana's in your rearview. You're headed for the big league now?" Brice finished his cocktail, and signaled for a refill. "Got your GPS set for the foremost veterinary orthopedic specialist on the East Coast." Brice gave Avery a shake, "They've been courting you like a virgin for a year. Then you play all hard to get running off to Mon-tan-a," he chewed each syllable like overcooked steak. "How long do you think you can string them along before they chase another tail?"

Avery shrugged off the unwanted clench. The details of the Maryland offer remained in an unopened envelope on the dresser in his room. He hadn't even glanced at the final proposal. Avery pushed his untouched cocktail aside.

"Inoculating horses, and building bionic limbs for crippled goats." Fueled by Avery's silence Brice elbowed the man next to him, "Wading through manure, birthing foals, castrating calf after calf... alluring work." He painted his derision painted with broad strokes. "Counted the days, I'd bet."

"Hours," Avery muttered. "I counted the hours."

Tory's knees weakened as Avery's words sliced through her. Escape was all she could think. She whirled in search of the nearest exit, and collided with a passing tray of cocktails. Her squeal of shock punctuated the sound of splintering glass, and cast the energetic room into silence.

Avery shook his head, certain she was an aberration. Despite wearing a tray of cocktails Tory was the most wonderful sight he'd seen in days. Her eyes, a mix of grief and embarrassment, met his for an instant.

Then she was gone.

CHAPTER FORTY-TWO

Tory's censure roared in her head. She made it as far as the lobby before Avery captured her arm.

"What are you doing here?"

"Don't worry," Tory yanked her elbow free, "in a few minutes, it'll be as if I never was."

"Tell that to the carpet in the ballroom."

Her face paled, and a single tear escaped.

Avery cursed his teasing, and guided a now pliable Tory around the corner. "I'm sorry," his arms wrapped tightly around her. She smelled like wine, and felt like heaven. "Thought I'd conjured you." His lips cruised over cheek and jaw, followed the line to her neck. She was here. Miles from her home, her obligations, she had come to him. He needed to get her out of the very public lobby, and up to his room.

It took a moment for Avery to realize she held her body rigid and unwelcoming. Balled fists, imprisoned between their chests pushed in an attempt for separation. "Avery…I have to go…I'm leaving."

He searched her face. Through tear tipped lashes, she held his gaze much like the wary mare he'd watched her rescue. Vulnerable and hurting. He feathered a touch over her arms. She shuddered.

Behind them the chime sounded announcing the elevator. Avery linked his fingers with hers and nudged until she was in the empty carriage. He released her hand long enough to press the button for his floor, then backed her against the rail, and waited as the door slid closed.

He leaned until his forehead rested against hers. "I'm so glad you're here," his whisper was tight with emotion. He kissed her damp cheeks, one, then the other. "But you aren't happy to see me."

Tory gripped his hips, and dragged him closer. Lifting her face she offered every unspoken word, as she touched her lips to his.

The elevator opened. Avery rotated them in a tangled dance along the corridor. He fumbled for his key, jammed the card into the slot, and urged the light to flash green. Shoving the door wide with his leg, Avery lifted her into the room, pinned her against the wall, and feasted on the flesh of her neck.

Tory shoved his coat off his shoulders. Pulled his shirt tails loose from his pants. Her busy hands tugged the knot of his tie, and unfastened the buttons on his shirt. Relentless, she shoved the material down his arms while her demanding mouth nipped his collarbone.

Hands sought and found flesh. She hitched higher locking her legs tight around his waist anchoring them together. Avery moaned, and pressed his hips home. Her eager fingers drifted lower and yanked at the buttons of her wine soaked blouse.

Madness, he thought, sweet, delicious, madness. Any shred of finesse evaporated as her shirt slipped off her shoulders and hit the floor. "Bed," he snarled, "we need a bed." Not willing to break contact, he gripped her thighs and carried her deeper into the room.

His knees bumped the mattress. He leaned, lowered, and followed her down.

The shower was running. Tory smiled as Avery started to sing. She gathered the sheet to her chest, and followed her impulse to join him. Giddy and slightly lightheaded, she eased off the mattress and noticed the thick binder on the dresser. Bold calligraphy graced the maroon leather. Tory ran her finger across the embossed letters. It was the proposal from the veterinary practice in Maryland. She cradled it like glass, and returned to the bed.

It was a horrific invasion of Avery's privacy. Shame and abhorrence united to boldly stain the fabric of her character. She opened the packet. The first page of the contract listed a triple digit salary, followed by a string of zero's.

The offer boggled Tory's mind. It was the kind of money which provided a life beyond dreams. No wonder Avery was thrilled.

Her heart plummeted. How could Doc Webb's small practice and county clinic compete? How could she?

Tory tossed the sheet aside, and searched for her scattered clothing. She picked up her ruined shirt and fastened the buttons. Tory twisted toward the mirror and cringed. Worse than the top, her hair was a tangled advertisement for a quality sleepless night. She raked her fingers through the strands.

The shower turned off.

Tory snagged Avery's hoodie, scooped up her shoes and purse, and fled.

She pulled the sweatshirt over her head, scurried down the hall, and into the elevator. She held her breath until the metal portal to freedom closed behind her. Tory punched the arrow for the lobby. The elevator paused on a lower floor. The doors opened and the loud-mouth from the ballroom got on. She lowered her gaze, dug her sunglasses from her purse, and slid them over her tear swollen eyes.

"Everything alright, sweetheart?" He angled closer, "I'd offer a tissue but I just finished a six-mile run, and a session of free weights." He chuckled, "I'd lend you my workout towel, but it is, after all, sweaty."

"No, thank you."

The elevator descended another few floors before Tory was alone in the carriage. It was barely daybreak. She decided to find a coffeehouse and pull herself together. Philadelphia certainly had enough to occupy her interest for the better part of the day. She'd sightsee until mid-afternoon then catch a late flight back to Montana.

After retrieving her luggage from the front desk, she moved to a quiet corner of the lobby. A wall of brochures captured her eye. Tourist highlights, tea houses, and historic bed-and-breakfasts in the area.

"Salsa," Tory groaned. "Damn it, Maggie."

CHAPTER FORTY-THREE

A vibrant woman opened the door and smiled. "Welcome, I'm Bethany. It's lovely to meet you, Tory."

"I apologize, Ms. Rush. I lost track of time."

"No worries, and call me Bethany. Leave your bags here in the foyer. I'm sure a shower and a quick rest would suit you. Maybe a light dinner?"

Bethany's gracious offer had Tory's stomach rumbling. "That's very generous, but I'm on standby for a flight west tonight."

"Pity. You must be exhausted from your travels. Avery tells me you were in Denver, then Kentucky, and now here touring the city."

"Yes, I've been away more than I've been home lately." Tory wandered into the living room.

"Did you enjoy the City of Brotherly Love? Authentic Philly cheesesteaks and Tastykakes. The Liberty Bell, and Independence Hall."

"I did, I guess," Bethany's question threw Tory. "I just wandered." She couldn't remember where she'd spent the hours. Her mind, full of Avery, had masked the history and architecture.

Tory walked to the window. Through the sheer panel of fabric she could see the children in the street. Like a movie scene they dragged a hockey goal into the quiet road to play their game. On occasion, a kid would shout 'CAR' and they would lug the apparatus to the safety of the sidewalk, and allow the vehicle to pass. Tory laughed as they hauled the portable field-of-play back into the center of the macadam. "Nice to see they want to be outside badly enough to persevere over the obstacles."

"Yes," Bethany joined her, "or a stern mother has kicked them out," she laughed. "I can remember bundling Avery in layers and shoving him into the first burst of springtime sun. All so I could enjoy an hour of peace, in a tidy kitchen."

Tory recalled her Nana doing the same when the weather grew less frigid.

"I hear you come bearing Maggie's delights."

"I do."

"How about I fix us some tea, and we have a sampling?"

"Sounds great," Tory relaxed for the first time since entering the home. "If you don't mind, maybe I will run upstairs, and freshen up."

Bethany's smile was radiant. "Top of the stairs and third door on your left. Everything you need should be on the washstand."

"Thank you, I'll be right down."

"No hurry," Bethany ducked into the kitchen, and sent a quick text message to her son.

Tory and Bethany sat in the dining room with a delicate china tea service between them. "This is lovely, but you didn't need to go to any trouble."

"The hospitality industry is my passion. I find fussing over the details relaxing."

"You and Maggie must be related," Tory reached into her satchel and handed the stack of recipe cards to Bethany.

"Oh," she handled the bundle with reverence. "Maggie is truly gifted. Do you have any favorites?"

"Unfortunately, I love everything Maggie makes. But today," Tory lifted a tiny powder dusted cookie and grinned, "these are my favorite."

"I'll be sure to send a few back with you."

"You must be excited for Avery's new job."

"I have to admit I'll enjoy having him close to home, not that three hours is next door."

"The Maryland practice is very prestigious."

"He's always known his own mind, rarely changes it once he's settled on something."

Tory smiled, "I'm familiar with the type."

"I'll tell you, it was clear this final rotation with Doc Webb made an impression. I could hear the satisfaction in his voice whenever we spoke."

"Doc Webb is a remarkable man."

"A father figure to you, right? Mentored you and your brother, Murphy is it?" Tory's brows raised in surprise. Bethany sipped her tea. "Avery's told me a great deal about you, and your ranch, and the work you do. He says you're a skilled healer."

Tory's mouth fell open, "I'm not sure how to respond."

"How about, thank you."

"I guess," Tory chuckled, "but Avery's not here at the moment."

"Actually…"

The swinging door connecting the dining room and kitchen opened. Avery stepped toward the table. His eyes awash with hurt, and confusion held Tory's. "Mom, this is Tory Keen."

"Yes honey, we've met." Bethany wiped her hands, and pushed from the table. "I'm off to play Bunco with the girls," she laid her hand on Avery's shoulder in reassurance. "Tory is expecting to catch a late flight. Talk her out of it. I've prepared the master on the second level." Bethany turned to Tory, "It was wonderful to meet you. I hope to see you at my table for breakfast."

"Well, I'm not..."

"No pressure, if not this trip, then the next. You couldn't possibly have seen everything Philadelphia has to offer."

"Thank you for the tea."

"Anytime," Bethany carried her cup and saucer toward the kitchen. "Oh Tory, please jot down Maggie's address, the postal kind, I'd like to send her a note." The swinging door closed at her back.

Avery stood rooted to the floor beside the table.

"Maggie wanted to share some recipes with your Mom, I wanted a chance to say goodbye... It was more secure, by Maggie's estimation, for me to hand deliver." She wasn't making any sense. Tory closed her eyes and willed him to stop looking at her.

"You left."

"I did," she couldn't concentrate with those blue eyes burrowing in. "I went to the hotel to see if you... If we... or I...I shouldn't have left the hotel without telling you, but honestly, Avery..." the syllables quivered.

"Why?"

"Complications, the real world kind." Tory's face flushed, as she shoved from the table. "Obstacles, opportunity, dreams, reality, geography," her hands tossed in anguish. "It's an ugly soup that can't be made palatable. Last night was ..."

"Perfect."

"A wonderful evening in a hotel room doesn't hold in the future," her shoulders fell in defeat. "Bubbles from a child's plastic wand in summertime...we're soapy water without the stick."

"What's between us is not soapy water."

She faced him with quiet tears threatening to spill. "I know...but we're floating at the wind's mercy, and I can't face the pop."

He closed the distance, laced his fingers through hers, "Stay, please... just tonight."

Her heart wouldn't survive it. "I need to call a cab."

"If you insist on leaving, I'll drive you."

"No, I can..."

"Tory," his breath hitched.

"Alright."

He held her hand the entire drive. His thumb circled lazily over the back of her knuckles as he eased into chaos at the terminal. "I'm going to call you," Avery stopped in the loading zone. "Please don't send every call to voicemail." He tugged her hand to his lips, "Text me, when you board, when you're home."

"I will," Tory's voice was a murmur of despair. She released his hand, reached over the seat, and pulled her duffle across her lap.

The taxi driver behind them blew the horn.

Tory leaned over, pressed her lips firmly to his. Her eyes stayed open, memorizing the endless chapters of unspoken words between them.

She lowered her head, and took a measured breath. When her gaze lifted she was collected and composed. She presented a polite and unruffled smile, gripped the handle, and without a word she exited the car.

CHAPTER FORTY-FOUR

An ambulance siren screamed as it carried some unfortunate soul toward healing hands. Avery lay awake and watched the shadows cast from the streetlamps paint his bedroom ceiling.

He hadn't convinced her to stay. Was it too much to wish Tory Keen would go soft and fall into his arms and beg him to change his plans?

Avery rolled and punched the pillow, kicked the comforter, and draped his leg over the side of the bed. She'd sent a text when she boarded, and any moment he'd receive another confirming her arrival in Montana.

His mother had come home. Accustomed to entering in virtual silence, she had retired to her room on the first floor. Avery should have left a note. He didn't want her to fuss over a breakfast for Tory.

He climbed from the bed. The invading city light washed across the dresser and reflected against gold leaf lettering. Beneath the rich burgundy binder another official proposal sat bound with less flair.

Two solid offers, but not apples to apples.

Avery flicked on the bedside lamp. Time to study them, side by side.

Avery jogged down the last five steps. His mom was at the stove whipping up a frittata. The table, set for three, hosted homemade granola and a plate of fresh fruit.

"Morning, Mom," Avery shifted past her, lifted the extra bowl and plate, and returned them to the cupboard.

Over her shoulder Bethany watched, "Just us?" At her son's 'uh huh', she filled a mug with fresh brewed coffee, set it on the table.

"I'm not hungry."

"Sit," Bethany coaxed him into a chair, topped off her own cup, and settled across from him.

Avery knew he wouldn't escape the kitchen without swallowing sustenance. He selected a kiwi, picked up a paring knife, and started to peel and chunk the fruit.

Bethany remained quiet. She answered the oven timer, and placed the piping hot egg dish on the counter to cool. The picture of patience, she returned to the table and muted any reaction when Avery scooped a serving of granola into his dish.

He wiped his mouth and pushed his empty bowl to the side. "You're sweating me out like you did when I was nine, and the garage window was broken."

She chuckled, "You certainly aren't in trouble, not the punishing kind anyway."

"You're disappointed."

"You know better than to tell me what I am." Bethany clucked her tongue. "You'll talk when you're ready." She walked his dish to the sink, and rested her hands on his tight shoulders. "I know you're sad, but until I know what's making you unhappy, I can't help. I certainly don't want to make it worse."

Avery rested his hand over her hers, then pulled her toward the chair. He ran hands over his face, placed his elbows on the table, and steepled his fingers. "The job I've always wanted and the city life that goes with it are happening," he sighed and lowered his palms to the table. "The experience with Doc Webb was inspirational. I was challenged in ways I'd never imagined." He picked up his napkin and put it down again. "The Montana lifestyle," he blew out a breath, "there couldn't be a bolder contrast to metropolitan living. The peace of the West...I don't know how to explain," his hands lifted at the loss of words. "My time spent there was like an everyday high which had little to do with altitude."

"And?"

"It's not what I've wanted all my life."

"You've made friends?"

"I made friends during every internship."

"Acquaintances, more than likely. People pass through our lives, add to our experiences and contribute pieces of who we become. Not everyone sticks."

"The people in Montana are lifelong friends. Doc Webb will be a trusted colleague, forever."

"And Tory?"

"She's so independent and smart. Strong in a way that intimidates, but isn't arrogant. She's not at all what I expected."

"Quite a woman."

"Yes."

"And?"

Avery sat quietly. "The life she's always wanted is happening for her in Montana."

"Advice time," Bethany reached across the table covered his hand with hers, "whether you want it, or not."

"Of course I do."

"Work is what links together the hours we serve in order to provide for the hours we savor. Infuse as much of what you truly love into your career. But above all," she smiled quietly, "I want you to choose the job which fortifies the man you want to become."

Chapter Forty-Five

The breezeway glass framed the season like an artist's work of genius. Vibrant green grass and cheeky budding wildflowers pushed through the frost hardened ground. The spring shoots were a delightful treat for the grazing horses after the cold winter. But even spring, Tory's favorite season since childhood, failed to lighten her mood.

It had been two weeks since Tory left Avery to begin the next phase of his life. He'd called and emailed but she saw little reason to prolong their liaison. Avery was beginning new, just like the pastures outside her window. Perhaps Tory needed something fresh.

The dogs pushed the door open to the main house. "Good morning, four leggers." She eased into the chair and accepted their pure affection. Poncho turned in a circle of happiness offering his back to Tory's rubbing fingers. "I can smell breakfast," she stood and allowed the dogs to lead the way.

"Good morning, Tory love," Ginny scooped a heaping ladle of oatmeal into a dish. "The day you arrive late to my kitchen…" Tory's smile was slow and sad. Ginny reached into the cupboard, "Add some nuts and cranberries. Why not go all out? I'll give you a splat of heavy cream."

Tory laughed then turned toward the foyer. Murphy and Riley's voices lifted in excited whispers. Ginny grabbed the tea towel, dried her hands, and followed Tory toward the noise.

On the second floor landing, Murphy straddled the banister while Riley stood close and listened intently.

Murphy released his weight and slid from the top all the way to the bottom.

"Awesome!" Riley exclaimed.

"Hush," Murphy chuckled. "This is supposed to be a quiet way to arrive on the first floor."

"I can be quiet." Riley threw his leg over the rail and breezed down the flight. Murphy plucked him from the bottom and swung his feet to the floor. "That's the only way to start your day." He ruffled the boy's mussed hair, and turned for the kitchen.

Riley pulled up short when he spotted Ginny, unsmiling, with her arms crossed sternly over her chest. "We might have stepped in the steaming pile, Dad." Riley's little hands reached back and wrapped Murphy's legs as he braced for a reprimand.

Tory peered over Ginny's shoulder and snickered at the mischievous pair.

"Boys," Ginny studied the guilty over the frame of her glasses. "Who's hungry?"

Murphy shook Riley's shoulder, "I am, how 'bout you?"

"Starved," Riley skipped to Ginny and slipped his hand in hers. "Banister sliding sparks a man's appetite."

Ginny allowed Tory to help her straighten the kitchen. The girl was wearing her melancholy like a pair of seasoned cowboy boots, regardless of how hard she pretended not to be miserable.

"Ginny, do you have a bucket list?"

"Store list? Cleaning supplies and such?"

"No," Tory grinned. "A wish list of things to do before you die, like skydiving, or traveling to an exotic location?"

"I'm not after jumping from a functioning aircraft, plus they video tape you on the way down. Do you have any comprehension of what seven decades of skin looks like falling sixty miles an hour?" Ginny recoiled in mock horror. "I'd like to meet Ellen DeGeneres. I'd like to see Ireland and Iceland, and eat pancakes at an IHOP."

"How about you, Tory love?"

"I have no idea, but I think it's time I work on one."

"I suggest you get to it. You have more days and stronger bones. Let me tell you, every day that passes you'll rethink the skydiving." Ginny closed the cupboard, removed her apron. "What about happily ever after? Is that on your hopes and dreams list?"

"Not sure you can purchase a ticket to everlasting love," sarcasm drenched Tory's words.

"Love can be beautiful, you know that. You've seen it with your own jaded eyes. Do you think Murphy's love for Jess will sour?"

"Not every man's as good as Murphy."

"True," Ginny softened her tone. "How about your grandparents?"

Tory's throat clogged as the memory filled her mind. Theirs had been love beyond measure. She worried with their example as her standard, she'd be destined to remain alone. "Fighting dirty."

"You aren't giving me much choice, as you've chosen to root yourself firmly in the camp of pessimists. You know how to love with your entire heart. You do it every day with those rescues. I've seen you lock lips with that llama every time he offers them to you."

Tory sniffed over her laugh. "The animals can't hurt me."

"True...great love risks great loss." Ginny rested her cheek on Tory's shoulder, "Never thought you were a chicken."

"I'm not," Tory puffed.

"But you are in this instance," Ginny said easily. "What's worse? You're selling yourself short." She allowed her words to hang in the air. "You're heading over to Maggie's tonight? If anyone can catalog a list of wild adventures, and tick off the tally, it'd be that girl."

Tory and Jess sat at the counter, a platter of fruit and cheese between them.

"Not hungry, Jess?" Maggie dropped spoonfuls of cookie batter on a tray.

"I'll have some grapes, in a minute."

"I'll have a sugar cake," Tory lifted a fluffy disk dusted with coarse sugar.

Maggie leaned away from the stove, "I'm with you. Who can say no?" She broke a cookie in half, set it on a napkin, and pushed the treat toward Jess. "Eat me, eat me," she tinkled with mirth. "They're Bethany's, by the way."

"It was really nice of her to share some recipes," Jess broke off a corner and tasted. "Wow, they are good."

"While we're all basking in sugar infused happiness, let's talk cakes." Maggie rinsed her fingers then cued up a file on her laptop. "I'm doing one for Doc and Mrs. Webb's reception."

"Hope it's not a naughty one," Tory frowned.

"Of course not, a traditional, two tier with fresh flowers." Maggie twirled the screen toward her friends.

"Oh Maggie," Jess's eyes filled. "That's beautiful."

"Easy Waterworks, it's dessert." Tory passed Jess a napkin to curb the tears.

"My cakes can hardly be described as a simple dessert."

"No offense," Tory raised her hands. "It looks big, how many guests?"

"One hundred fifty."

"What?" Tory sputtered.

"Catered the full shebang, half the county's invited. Polish your smile Jess, Murphy will be introducing you and Riley all night long. I plan to be shined up and sparkling for the hot and randy ranchers."

"You know all of them already," Tory bit into another sugar cake. "Not all, plus there's bound to be a surprise or two hiding on Doc Webb's family tree. Ripe for the pickin'," she rubbed her hands with glee.

"Joel's coming," Tory tossed the barb and immediately regretted shoving her bad mood on Maggie.

Jess clapped, "And he's staying to celebrate Riley's birthday."

"Speaking of the birthday boy," Maggie's gaiety returned as she tapped the keys. "Your boy, ten years old... no trains, dinosaurs, or Ninja turtles."

"Not for Riley," Jess laughed. "He'd like the zombie apocalypse."

"A challenge, I love it," Maggie beamed, "the undead which still looks tasty enough to eat."

Chapter Forty-Six

Tory dressed the part, even though she felt like shedding the fabric and crawling into bed. She was becoming a pro at masking her feelings. It was exhausting. Tory studied her reflection in the full-length mirror, and forced her lips to curve upward. If anyone was worth her mustering a front of false happiness, it was Doc Webb and his wife.

"Where's my hot date?" Joel's voice bellowed.

Tory chuckled and grabbed her clutch. "Just putting on the finishing touches."

"Well quit, you're a knockout." Joel raised his index finger and circled it in the air asking for a turn. Tory indulged him by spinning quickly enough to have the hem of her dress fluttering, in soft waves, mid-thigh.

"God bless designers," he walked toward her, caught her hand and pulled her close. "You're so gorgeous. Marry me."

Tory hugged him, "You are so good for my ego."

"Ready?"

"As I'm going to get."

***

The Webb house was packed with guests. A projection screen flipped through images from the anniversary trip. People joked about Doc Webb's tan lines, and inquired about his retirement.

Doc Webb's cheeks were flushed and, tucked beneath his arm, his wife wore a dazzling expression of the truest love. Champagne corks popped and the toasts began.

Tory stood on the fringe of the festivities. As predicted, Murphy introduced Jess and Riley, and Maggie flirted with the men of Taylor Ranch.

"Great party," Joel joined Tory and handed her a glass of punch.

"Told you it'd be worth the trip," she accepted the glass. Applause rang out, and guests lifted their glasses in cheers.

"Sip slowly," he warned. "It's got a fierce kick."

Maggie's laughter floated above the din. Every time Joel had maneuvered in her direction she'd found an interest on the opposite side of the room.

He grumbled, "Who's on the receiving end of Maggie's attention now?"

Tory tipped her head and studied Joel, "Could be you, if you'd stop being a weenie."

"I thought forty years was ruby," Joel shifted topics. "What's the deal with the origami?"

Tory looked closely at the glass dishes sprinkled throughout the room. She realized each was filled with small silver triangles. "Gum wrappers," she whispered over the clutch in her chest.

"Trash?"

"Not trash," her voice wavered. "Love in the purest of form."

It was the final pebble. Tory had reached the summit of her acting ability. Emotional control toppled and rushed down the mountainside in an avalanche of chaos. She pushed her drink into Joel's hands, and hurried through the room. She'd find Murphy and Jess, and ask them to make her apologies.

She saw them tucked in a quiet corner across the room. Their heads were nestled together in a private secret. Tory watched as her brother lifted two glasses of champagne from a passing tray, drained half the sparkling champagne from one cup, then offered it to his wife. Jess's hesitation was brief, her smile glowing as Murphy tucked a stray hair behind her ear.

The sweetness ripped Tory's tattered emotions. Murphy eased closer, his hand trailed over Jess's arm until his open palm rested over her abdomen.

A painful punch stole Tory's breath. Pregnant.

She covered her keening gasp with a cough and stumbled backwards toward the kitchen. She dodged the catering staff, and burst onto the porch. The fresh night air stung her eyes. Numb hands grasped blindly for the railing as the clapping from the latest toast permeated the walls and windows.

Everyone moving forward…she was standing still. Tory was satisfied with her life. Murphy had been too, a short time ago. Only a fool could see how his happiness had multiplied with the additions of Jess and Riley, and now a baby.

Jellied legs hurried toward the truck, only to realize the hasty exit left her without coat, keys, and purse. Across the driveway, the little cottage Avery had called home sat empty. She walked to the door and gripped the handle, the knob turned.

Tory pushed inside, closed out the night. With her back pressed against the solid wood, she loosened her knees, slid to the floor, and allowed the wave of agony to drown her.

Maggie rushed toward the small house. The torrent of pain reached her ears before she'd placed her foot on the porch. Maggie leaned her forehead against the door and waited for a break in the raging storm. She eased the door open. Tory looked broken. Mascara streaked her cheeks. Her nose was red and raw. "How can I help?"

She sniffed, "Give me your car."

Avery navigated the sea of guests. He found Doc Webb, and gripped his hand, "Congratulations."

"You made it." A dazed Doc Webb hooked his wife's arm, "Look honey, it's Avery. Sorry kid, bourbon makes me sappy." He grasped Avery's shoulder, "Wife put fresh sheets in the apartment. Make yourself at home for as long as you'd like."

"Thank you."

"Get a drink. It's a night for celebrating."

Avery grabbed a cocktail then spotting Murphy and Jess, he moved across the room to greet them.

"What a wonderful surprise," Jess hugged him.

With less enthusiasm, Murphy offered a polite handshake, and then gestured to a man at his side. "Joel, this is Avery, the intern who filled in for Webb."

"Great to meet you."

Avery gripped Joel's hand. "I admire your design on Tory's cottage."

"He's seen Tory's cottage?" Joel's speculative gaze drifted to Murphy's, "the inside?"

Maggie sauntered over and slid her arm neatly though Avery's. "Welcome back, handsome," she purred and kissed his cheek.

"Wow, you look beautiful."

Maggie was pleased to see the muscle jump along Joel's jaw. She traced her hand over the bodice of her dress, "This rag?" Her laughter trilled.

Joel's teeth set on edge. She flirted with every man in the place, while ignoring him.

Avery leaned close, lowered his voice. "Where's Tory?"

Maggie trailed a single finger over Avery's forearm, "I'd be happy to help you with that. Follow me." She gripped his hand, and dragged him from the room.

Once on the porch, flirt flashed to fire. Maggie shoved her hands against Avery's chest and launched him back a full step. "What the devil do you think you're doing?" She stalked toward him. "This is not a game, and Tory is not some tartlet you can nibble on until you decide if the flavor suits your pallate."

"Maggie, I...um... I didn't mean."

"Men never intend, but they twist and they play, and leave us floundering like laundry on a windy day."

"Where's Tory?" Avery repeated.

"She left, and she's miserable, though she pretends not to be. You leave her alone."

A rush of party noise halted Maggie's verbal assault. Joel stepped on the porch and pulled the door closed behind him. "Avery, if you wouldn't mind, I need a moment with Maggie."

Avery had already taken advantage of the distraction and was making a hasty retreat.

Maggie spun toward Joel, "You had no business running him off." She squealed as Joel closed the distance. "I may spend my time doing ..."

"Whatever you want," he cut her off, "with anyone you want. Half the county and from what I understand, thanks to the internet, you're now accessible to the entire world."

Maggie's mouth dropped wide. "I'm free, and available."

"Not tonight, you're not," he blocked her in.

She backed up, and bumped into the porch swing. "Joel, I'm not interested in being your Midwestern convenience."

She might have delivered a sharp blow to his kidneys. Breath whooshed past his lips, "Maggie, I never meant for you to feel..."

"How I feel is my problem," pride straightened her spine. "I'm not available to you tonight." She marched toward the steps, and realized her car had left with Tory. She faltered and then turned toward the front door.

"Maggie," Joel's voice was tender, as he hooked her elbow.

"No," she shook her head. "Please don't."

He felt her tremble, "You matter to me."

Tory's sobs still echoed in her heart. If Maggie wasn't careful she'd end up wrecked just like her friend. She placed her hand over Joel's and freed her arm, "It's time I matter to me more."

CHAPTER FORTY-SEVEN

Tory wrapped up her pity party on the drive home. If her face hadn't been ruined she might have returned to the celebration.

Liar, fraud, fake, her alter ego skewered her with a trio of well aimed jibes.

She navigated her dark cottage, stripped out of her fancy dress, then pulled on soft pants. Even though it weakened her, Tory tugged Avery's hoodie over her head. The little champagne she'd tasted swam in her belly like an undesirable guest. She stopped in the kitchen and grabbed a sleeve of saltines. Remi plodded into the room and leaned her body against Tory's thigh.

"Hi, pretty lady," she stroked her fur. "Should've stayed home with you tonight. It's not nice to be force-fed sweetness with a side of undying love when you're feeling sorry for yourself." Tory reached for the open bottle of red wine, then switched to the refrigerator and removed the pitcher of iced tea. "I don't want to be numb," she explained to Remi as she poured a tall glass. "Need to feel every ache, so the hurt loses the muscle to kick my teeth out."

Tory walked to the breezeway, flipped on the ceramic heater, and settled into the rocking chair. Toes pushed and the gentle sway soothed. Remi stretched across the floor, propped her chin on her master's feet. The simplicity of the dog's love walloped the barrier Tory had erected on the drive home. Tears coursed down her cheeks. She melted from the chair to the chilled floor. Remi shifted and climbed into Tory's lap.

Avery parked behind the barn in hope of avoiding the dogs. Through the glass he saw her. He absorbed the wash of contentment at the sight. Tory seated on the floor with the dog's tail thumping in response to something she'd said.

He watched as she shifted, clambered to her feet, plucked a tissue from the box and wiped her face. Her beautiful features were tinted with anguish and pain.

Would he make it better or worse? Maggie's warning made him hesitate and re-evaluate his decision to contact Tory tonight. Slowly, he retreated into the shadow of the house.

Remi barked, and danced in delighted circles at Tory's feet. "Wanna go out?" She pushed the door open, and startled when movement snagged her peripheral vision. For an instant her imagination, increasingly cruel, twisted the dark into the figure she longed to see.

Remi raced toward the shape. The silhouette shifted and became flesh and blood.

"Tory, it's me," Avery strode across the dew soaked grass.

Her vision adjusted to the dark, and settled on the fancy clothes. The reception, her heart plummeted. He was here for Doc Webb's party.

"Come on, Remi, inside," she called the dog, and turned toward her house.

"Tory," Avery hurried to intercept. She wouldn't dismiss him, not tonight. His hand snaked out and captured her arm.

"I've had a long night, Avery. You should head over to the reception. Doc Webb will be thrilled you made the trip."

"I've been to the party."

"You didn't fly all the way out here to duck out on the event of the season. They'll celebrate until dawn and rumor has it, Mrs. Webb laid out a fortune for a breakfast buffet with made-to-order omelets."

"Sounds tasty but," his quiet eyes focused on her, "I'm pretty sure the celebration I'm interested in attending is happening right here, at Keen Ranch."

Tory studied him, "I'm cold, and I'm tired. Frankly, I've enjoyed all the turmoil I can handle for one evening."

Avery slipped his coat off and wrapped it around her shoulders. He fingered the material of his college sweatshirt, "I blamed the maid for stealing this."

Tory's cheeks flushed, "I was going to get it back to you. No, that's a lie, a bold fat lie, I'm keeping it. You can buy another one."

He laughed, "I think I like it better on you."

"Avery," Tory faltered. If she didn't get some separation she'd fall into the chasm all over again.

"This will only take a minute, but I need you outside." He chuckled when she resisted, "Always the hard way." Avery scooped her off her feet and into his arms. "Woman, be still, or you'll throw my back out. Not that I'd discourage your oiled hands rubbing me anywhere you'd like."

Tory sucked in a breath and prepared to launch her protest. Avery turned his head cutting off her words most effectively with his mouth. She fought for a half a second, then her resistance thawed, and ended on a moan.

Avery released her legs, grappled to pull her closer. He trailed his lips over her cheeks and tear swollen eyes. "I don't like to see you unhappy."

"You aren't responsible for all of it."

"That's a relief," he smiled and ran his thumbs along her jaw. "I have a few things to tell you." He pressed his lips to her forehead. "Works out well for me that you refuse to answer your email. Some news is better in person."

Tory eased back.

"I quit my job."

"You what?"

"You were right. Dream opportunities look very different when they're served up on a platinum platter. Don't fret, it turns out a certain Montana vet's ready to go part-time." He kissed her nose, "But that's not the party I'm inviting you to."

"It's not?"

He silenced her again. The kiss spiraled until both were breathless.

Slowly, Avery lowered to the damp meadow until he kneeled before her. His face tipped to hers. "Some dreams are at the foot of the mountain, in a place you never planned to visit, with a woman who is bold, and independent, and beyond beauty." His hand abandoned her hip to reach into his pocket.

Tory's breath clogged in her throat.

Moonbeams highlighted a brilliant channel-set diamond band. Avery gathered her left hand, "The Webbs are celebrating forty years," he kissed her knuckles. "How do you feel about taking a run at sixty?"

The jeweled circle glided over her ring finger and rested against her hand. Tory closed her eyes and savored the emotions racing through her. She angled her head to the side and smiled, "Are you sure your thin East Coast hide can handle a raw Montana winter?"

"We'll take tropical vacations," Avery drew her down. "Is that a yes?"

Tory nodded and pressed her lips gently to his, "Yes."

Avery gathered her close, "Do you want to head over to the party, share the news, and get in line for an omelet?"

She eased back and traced her finger tips over his jaw. "No, I think I'd rather be late for breakfast."

OTHER TITLES BY THE AUTHOR

Falling in love with my characters is a wonderful weakness… I first introduced Tory Keen on the pages of *Saltwater Cowboy*. Devoted sister to Murphy, Tory encourages him to take a vacation and champions his heart when he finds more than relaxation on the sandy shores of Chincoteague, Virginia.

Don't miss book one ~ Murphy and Jess's sweet summer romance ~ *Saltwater Cowboy*. More than sand shifts beneath Murphy's cowboy boots when he meets Jess, an island naturalist, during the Wild Pony Penning on Chincoteague Island, Virginia.

Invisible Woman ~ inspirational fiction ~ a thought provoking celebration of friendship awaits when Jillian, Arie, and Sarah attend the Awakening Goddess Retreat and uncover pure joy and embrace their inner radiance.

"Here's the Thing…" ~ humorous fiction ~ a thrill ride of delightfully destructive mishaps overtakes a family wedding weekend where the only life preserver 'for better or for worse' is bloodline.

CONNECT WITH LAURA

Digital reviews go a long way in helping me reach new readers!
I invite you to join me online and spread the love through any
and every social media shouting box you have.

Facebook.com/LauraRudacille

Twitter.com - @LRudacille

Blog - http://laurarudacille.com/